CHINESE
GHOST STORIES
for Language Learners

Author: Pinglan Mo
Translator: Amy Lin

探索古中国的鬼魅传说。

陪你走进恐怖世界，

Introduction

In this collection, we have carefully curated 15 intriguing ghost or supernatural stories, presented in both Chinese and English. These stories are new adaptations of selected tales from renowned literary works in China, including *Strange Tales from a Chinese Studio* 《聊斋志异》, *Miscellaneous Morsels from Youyang* 《酉阳杂俎》, *Anecdotes About Spirits and Immortals* 《搜神记》, and more.

Why Do We Adapt These Stories?

We adapt these stories for a couple of reasons. First, classic Chinese literature is often written in a style that differs significantly from modern Chinese, posing challenges for contemporary readers. Second, some of these works serve not merely as entertainment but as records of extraordinary events and folklore, employing straightforward language without elaborate storytelling. Our new adaptations preserve the original plots while presenting them in modern standard Mandarin with a more engaging narrative. This approach allows readers to enjoy the stories while learning common and useful vocabulary and expressions.

Key Terms to Learn about Chinese Mythology, Beliefs, and Culture

While the stories have been adapted and written in modern Chinese, some concepts and values the stories convey may still be difficult for Chinese learners to understand as they require knowledge of Chinese history, mythology, beliefs, and culture. As a result, at the end of each story, we have included bilingual explanations of key terms to help our readers better understand the story, enrich their reading experience, and explore Chinese mythology, beliefs, and culture.

The Advantage of Reading Bilingual Stories

The most beneficial advantage of reading bilingual stories is being able to observe the grammatical, literal, and cultural nuances between the two languages. When translating these stories from Chinese to English for educational purposes, the resulting translation isn't always precise or "beautiful." Sometimes, instead of providing a more authentic or literary translation in English, we preserve the original Chinese sentence structures. At other times, particularly concerning Chinese idioms and expressions, we prioritize conveying their meaning rather than translating them literally. By observing these subtle differences, readers will train themselves to think in Chinese.

Stories Told in a Specific Order

To help readers better understand the Chinese view on spirits and ghosts, these 15 stories cover a variety of topics and are told in a specific order. The first three stories are about how evil spirits disturb humans. Followed by Stories 4, 5, and 6 on how humans transform into ghosts. Then Stories 8, 9, and 10 explain how and why animals, plants, and even inanimate objects acquire supernatural abilities. Stories 11, 12, and 13 delve into what the underworld is like in Chinese beliefs and how it works. Finally, the last two stories explore the concept of reincarnation.

Furthermore, in these stories, you will find spirits and ghosts that are widely known in China, such as 画皮鬼 (The Ghost with Painted Skin), 狐狸精 (The Fox Spirit), 钟馗 (Zhong Kui), etc.

Upon finishing the book, readers will have gained a fundamental grasp of the Chinese perspective on spirits and ghosts. This knowledge not only enhances their appreciation of Chinese cinema and literature but also offers insights into Chinese culture.

CONTENTS

目录

鬼压床

The Ghost Pressing Down on the Bed

本页插图选自《亿春书瑞图》，清代 刘权之 绘，现藏于台北故宫博物院。

一个寻常的夏日午后，一老头吃过午餐感觉有点困倦。他离开饭桌，留他妻子一个人在院子里洗碗，他走进房间里躺下睡午觉。

也不知道睡了多久，他迷迷糊糊地睁开了眼睛，看见一个女人走进屋里来。这个女人年纪大约有30多岁，头上裹着白布，身上穿着丧服。她进来后就直接向里面的房间走去，好像在寻找什么人。

老头猜想，这个女人可能是同村的，吃过午饭没事做，来找自己的妻子聊天的吧。可是他转念一想，村里没有人过世啊，这女的为什么穿着丧服？就算她的亲人去世了，她也不能穿着丧服跑到别人家里来，这多不吉利啊！

正在他猜疑不定的时候，那个女子从里面的房间走了出来。老头这才仔细看清她的脸。她面色发黄，整张脸都肿肿的，她眉头紧锁，一丝笑容都没有，神情十分可怕。她在房间里走来走去，看起来还是在寻找着什么。

老头把眼睛微微闭了起来，稍微留下一点缝隙，他想看看这个女人到底想干什么。

On an ordinary summer afternoon, an old man felt a bit sleepy after having lunch. He left the dining table, leaving his wife alone in the courtyard washing dishes. He walked into the room to lie down to take a nap.

Not sure how long he had slept, he opened his eyes hazily and saw a woman walk into the room. This woman was around 30-something years old. She had a white fabric on her head and wore mourning clothes. After coming inside the house, she walked directly to the room in the back and seemed to be searching for someone.

The old man assumed that the woman was probably from the same village, had lunch, and had nothing to do so she came over to chat with his wife. However, he then had another thought. No one had passed away in the village. Why was the woman wearing mourning clothes? Even if her relative passed away, she shouldn't come to other people's houses wearing mourning clothes. That was ominous!

As he was doubting and uncertain, that woman came out of the back room. The old man was then able to see her face clearly. Her complexion was yellow, and her entire face was swollen. Her brows were tightly furrowed, no trace of a smile, and her facial expression was terrifying. She walked back and forth in the room as if still searching for something.

The old man closed his eyes lightly, leaving just a small crack as he wanted to see what this woman wanted to do.

没过一会儿，女子靠近了他的床，在床边盯着他看了一会儿，突然爬上了床，整个人坐在了老头的肚子上。她非常沉重，根本不像是一个人的体重。老头甚至觉得她有上千斤重。他想伸手推开这女人，但是发现自己的手好像被捆住了一样，根本动不了。他又试着抬腿，发现腿也仿佛瘫痪了一样，毫无知觉。他急忙张口呼救，可他也发不出声音来。

这时候，那个女子把头靠近老头的脸，开始用鼻子来闻他。从额头，眉毛，眼睛，鼻子一点点地挨个闻过去。老头感觉女人鼻子里和嘴里呼出来的气冷得像冰一样。他冷得浑身都是鸡皮疙瘩，那阵阵寒气似乎渗入到骨头里去了。虽然不知道理由是什么，老头觉得继续这样下去，他的命就要保不住了。情急之中，他想到了一个方法。

等到女人的鼻子一点点向下移动，闻到老头的嘴的旁边时，老头突然张口咬住了女子的脸，他用尽浑身力气，拼命咬着不松口，感觉牙齿都陷进肉里去了。那女子痛得一边挣扎一边尖叫。老头仍然不肯松口，血液从女子的脸颊上不住地往下流。

Not too long after, the woman came closer to his bed and stared at him next to his bedside for a while. Then she crawled up on the bed suddenly and sat on the old man's stomach. She was very heavy. It did not feel like the body weight of one person. The old man even felt that she was at least over 500 kilograms. He wanted to extend his hands to push the woman off. But he noticed that he couldn't move his hands at all, as if something tied them down. He tried to raise his legs, but his legs were not responding, as if they were paralyzed. He hurriedly opened his mouth trying to call for help, but no sound came out.

At this time, the woman drew her head close to the old man's face and started using her nose to sniff him. From his forehead to his eyebrows, eyes, and then to his nose, sniffing one little section at a time. The old man felt that the air that came out from the woman's nose and mouth was as cold as ice. It was so cold that he got goosebumps all over his body. The wave of cold air felt like they were seeping into his bones. Although he wasn't sure what the reason was, the old man felt that if he let this continue, he would lose his life. In a state of urgency, he came up with a solution.

The old man waited till the woman's nose had moved down a bit and got next to his mouth, then the old man suddenly opened his mouth and bit the woman's face. He used all his strength, clamping onto it relentlessly. It felt like his teeth were sinking into the flesh. The woman was in so much agony that she was struggling and screaming at the same time. The old man refused to let go, and blood continued to flow down from the woman's cheek.

正在双方陷入僵局不分胜负时，老头忽然听到院子里妻子说话的声音。他赶紧大声呼救："有鬼！"但他这一松口，那女子就飞一般地逃走了。老头的身体也恢复了知觉，等他坐起来时，女人已经消失不见。

他妻子听到呼喊声立刻走进屋来。老头问她看见一个女人出去了吗？妻子回答说没有。听了老头详细地描述了这件事之后，妻子笑他说肯定是做噩梦了。老头说不对，他感觉嘴里还有血腥味儿。他们一起查看四周，发现枕头的一边已经被血水湿透，老头的嘴上也还留有血迹，他越想越恶心，大口呕吐起来。他这可真是被鬼压身了啊！

本故事改编自《聊斋志异》里的短篇故事《咬鬼》（作者：蒲松龄，生卒年代: 1610年-1715年）

As the two of them struggled and came to a stalemate, the old man suddenly heard his wife's voice from the courtyard. He hurried and screamed for help, "There's a ghost!" But as soon as he let go of his grip, the woman quickly fled. The old man also regained his senses. When he sat up, the woman had already disappeared without a trace.

His wife heard the scream and immediately stepped inside. The old man asked if she saw a woman going out. His wife answered no. After hearing the old man's detailed description of what happened, his wife smiled and said he for sure had a nightmare. The old man said that wasn't true because he could still feel the bloody taste in his mouth. They examined the surroundings together and noticed that a side of the pillow was soaked in blood. The old man's mouth also had a trace of blood. The more he thought about it, the more disgusted he felt, and he threw up heavily. He was really being pressed down by a ghost!

This story is an adaptation of the short story "Biting Ghost" from *Strange Tales from a Chinese Studio*. Author: Pu Songling, 1610-1715.

【鬼压床 guǐ yā chuáng】

鬼压床，又称鬼压身，指的是在睡觉的时候头脑突然有了意识，但是身体却不能动，有的人甚至还会出现幻觉。在现代医学里，人们把这种现象叫做睡眠瘫痪症。但是在中国古代，人们碰到这样的情况时会认为这是鬼压在了自己身上。即便在现代中国，也依然有人相信鬼的存在，所以也有很多人仍旧相信鬼压床。

"The ghost pressing down on the bed" or "the ghost pressing down on one's body" refers to the sudden gaining of consciousness during sleep, but the body is unable to move. Some people may even have hallucinations. In modern medicine, people call this phenomenon "sleep paralysis." However, in ancient China, people thought that a ghost was pressing down on one's body when this situation happened. Even in modern China, there are still people who believe in the existence of ghosts, so even now some people still believe in "a ghost pressing down on the bed."

【丧服 sāng fú】

对死者表示哀悼而穿的服装。如果有人去世了，他的亲戚们就需要穿上特殊的服装，去操办他的葬礼。这种特殊的服装就叫丧服。在中国古代，丧服皆为白色。在现代中国，传统葬礼越来越少，对丧服的要求也越来越少，只要是白色，黑色或者其他朴素的服装即可。

在中国古代，如果家里有人死了，那么穿着丧服待在自己的家里是正常的。但是，如果穿着丧服去别人家，会被认为是很没有礼貌的事情，因为这不吉利，就好像别人家里也会有人死掉。

Mourning attire is clothing people wear to express their grief for the deceased. If a person passes away, their relatives have to wear special clothing to handle his funeral. This kind of special clothing is called Sangfu (mourning attire). In ancient China, Sangfu was white. In modern China, traditional funerals are held fewer and fewer, so the requirement for Sangfu has become less strict. As long as the Sangfu is white, black, or other plain clothes, then it is acceptable.

In ancient China, if someone died in a family, then it was normal for the family members of the deceased to wear Sangfu in their own family. However, if the person wearing Sangfu went to other people's houses, then it was considered a rude gesture because it was ominous as if someone in the other family might also die.

图片摄于2023年，中国云南大理

图片描述：
一支送葬的队伍走过大理古城的街头，队伍中身穿白色丧服的人们是死者的直系亲属。

10

画皮
The Ghost with Painted Skin

本页插图选自《聊斋全图》第八册，清光绪时期绘本，现藏于奥地利国家图书馆。

很久以前，在山西太原有一个叫做王生的男人，他家境不错，住在一所大宅子里，还娶了一位既漂亮，又知书达礼的女人做妻子，生活幸福美满。

有一天早上，他不知道为什么很早就醒来，然后再也睡不着了，于是他决定一个人出门去散步。在家附近遇到了一位秀美的女子。这个女子背着个不小的包袱，独自一人急匆匆地赶路。王生见她貌美如花，不禁春心萌动，他走向前去拦住女子，问她："天还没亮，你一个女子怎么孤零零地走在路上？不害怕吗？"

那女人说："你是一个路过的行人，既不认识我，又不能替我分担忧愁，你问那么多干什么呢？"

王生不肯放女人离开，又说："你有什么忧愁呢？你告诉我，说不定我可以帮你呢。"

女子叹了口气，她眼泪汪汪，一脸悲伤地说："我家是穷苦人家。父母贪图钱财，把我卖给一个有钱的老头当他的小妾。这老头的正妻嫉妒我的美貌，经常骂我，打我。我实在忍受不了了，所以就凌晨偷跑出来，准备逃得远远的。"

A long time ago, in Taiyuan, Shanxi, there was a man named Wang Sheng. He was from a well-off family. He lived in a big house and married a wife who was not only beautiful but also well-educated. He had a happy life.

One day in the morning, for some reason, he woke up early and couldn't fall back asleep. So he decided to go out alone for a walk. Near his house, he ran into a beautiful woman. This woman carried a bag that wasn't small, walking alone in a hurry on the road. Wang Sheng saw that the woman was as beautiful as a tender flower. He couldn't help but feel attracted to her. He walked toward the woman to stop her, and asked her, "It is not even dawn yet. Why is a lady like yourself walking alone on the road? Aren't you scared?"

That woman said, "You are just a passerby. You don't know me nor can you help me with my worries. Why are you asking so many questions?"

Wang Sheng didn't let the woman leave, and spoke again, "What are your worries? Tell me, I might be able to help."

The woman sighed. Her tears welled in her eyes, looking deeply sad as she said, "I am from a poor family. My parents, greedy for money, sold me to a rich old man to be his concubine. The old man's wife is jealous of my beauty, often insults me, and beats me. I couldn't bear it any longer, so I ran away in the early morning, planning to escape as far as I could."

王生问道："你准备逃到哪里去呢？"

Wang Sheng asked, "Where are you planning to escape to?"

女子说："这世界上没人能帮助我，我也不知道能逃到哪里，逃到什么时候。"说完便低声哭了起来。

The woman said, "In this world, no one can help me. I don't know where I can escape to either, or when I can stop running away." As soon as she finished her words, she started sobbing softly.

王生看她楚楚可怜，主动提出帮助："我家离这里不远，你如果愿意的话，可以到我家里去。"

Seeing how pitiful she looked, Wang Sheng offered to help, "My house is not too far from here. If you are willing, you can go to my house."

女人很高兴地同意了。王生帮她拿着包袱，领她一起回了家。他担心妻子不开心，就把女子带到院子里的书房，让她在那里住了下来。

The woman happily agreed. Wang Sheng helped her carry her luggage and headed home with her. Wang Sheng worried that his wife might be unhappy, so he brought the woman to the study room in the courtyard, letting her live there.

就这么过了几天，王生的妻子知道了这件事，想要赶走那女人。女人哭着说："请不要赶我走，如果我被抓到了，一定会没命的。只要能让我活下去，我什么都愿意做，当先生的小妾或者仆人我都愿意。"

Just like that, a few days passed. Wang Sheng's wife found out about the woman and wanted to kick her out. The woman said while crying, "Please don't kick me out. If I get caught, I will definitely die. As long as I can survive, I am willing to do anything, whether it is to be master's concubine or servant."

王生不顾妻子的反对，执意继续收留女人。甚至那天晚上，他就来到女人的房间，一夜缠绵之后，他就更舍不得女人离开了。

Wang Sheng, disregarding his wife's objections, persisted in providing shelter for the woman. That very night, he went to the woman's room, and after a night of intimacy, he found himself even more reluctant to let the woman leave.

第二天，王生去拜访朋友，在街上他遇见了一个道士。那道士看到王生的脸，十分吃惊地说："你最近是不是遇到了什么奇怪的人呢？"王生说："没有呀！"道士又说："你全身都被邪气缠绕着，肯定是遇到恶鬼了。"王生仍然坚持说没有。道士只好离开，边走还边感叹说："死到临头了还如此执迷不悟。"

听了道士的话，王生不免有些怀疑那个女子。只是，昨夜和她云雨的画面还历历在目，她明明是个美艳的女郎，怎么可能是恶鬼呢？他想，一定是这道士骗他，想要借口帮他除掉恶鬼来骗他的钱财。

正胡思乱想着，他不知不觉地走回了家，走到了书房的门口。他发现大门从里面锁了起来，感觉有些奇怪。他蹑手蹑脚地来到窗前，向里面偷看。这一看差点吓得他叫出声来。只见一个怪物正对着镜子梳妆，它面目狰狞，脸色发青，牙齿又尖又长。它慢慢地理好自己的长发。然后把一张人皮铺在床上，拿起彩色的画笔认真地描绘：柳叶眉，含情脉脉的眼睛，樱桃般的小口……

The next day, Wang Sheng went to visit his friend. On the street, he ran into a Taoist monk. The monk was very surprised when he saw Wang Sheng's face, "Have you encountered any strange person lately?" Wang Sheng said, "No!" The monk spoke again, "You are surrounded by an evil aura. You must have encountered an evil demon." Wang Sheng insisted he didn't. The monk had no choice but to leave. He exclaimed while he walked, "Still so stubborn and not willing to come to senses even at the brink of death."

After hearing what the monk had said, Wang Sheng inevitably became a bit suspicious of that woman. It was just that the memory of their intimate encounter from the previous night was still fresh and vivid in his mind. She was clearly a beautiful lady. How could she possibly be an evil demon? He thought it had to be the monk wanting to deceive him and was using an excuse to help him get rid of evil demons to swindle money from him.

Lost in wild thoughts, he unconsciously arrived home and found himself at the entrance to the study room. He noticed that the door was locked from the inside. He found that strange. He tiptoed to the window, secretly peeking inside. This glance scared him so much that he almost screamed. He saw a monster looking in the mirror while brushing its hair. It had a ferocious appearance, with a green complexion and teeth that were sharp and long. It slowly brushed its long hair. Then it put a human skin on the bed, picked a color brush pen, and carefully drew: beautiful arched eyebrows, sparkling eyes, a mouth as small as a cherry...

画完后，它举起人皮，像穿衣服一样把人皮披在身上，于是就变成了那个美丽的女子。

王生亲眼看到这个场景后，万分恐惧，他紧咬着嘴唇，不敢发出一点声响，手脚并用地逃了出去。他疯了一般地跑到刚才碰见道士的地方，但那道士早就不知去向。他寻遍了所有的道观，终于在郊外的一处道观见到了那道士。一见面，王生就跪倒在地上，向道士讲述他刚才的可怕经历。

道士听后告诉王生，他刚才看到的怪物叫做画皮鬼，她原本也是寻常人家的女子，因为丈夫变了心，她郁郁而终。死后，她就变成了厉鬼，专门诱惑已经结了婚的男人，等到这个男人变了心，抛弃了自己的妻子，她就会挖开男人的胸膛，吃掉他的心脏。

王生求他救自己一命。道士交给王生一道符咒，告诉他把符咒挂在卧室的门口，就能赶走画皮鬼。

到了晚上，王生躲进卧室不敢睡觉。忽然，他听到门外响起了脚步声，那声音就在门口徘徊。

After it finished drawing, it picked up the human skin, and put it on as if wearing a piece of clothing, and as a result turning into that beautiful woman.

Wang Sheng saw the scene with his own eyes and became extremely frightened. He tightly bit his lips, not daring to make any sound. He fled using both his hands and feet. He ran like a maniac to the place where he met the monk earlier. But the monk had already disappeared. He searched through all the Taoist temples and eventually found that monk at a temple on the outskirts. As soon as he saw the monk, Wang Sheng knelt on the ground and recounted his frightening experience that just happened to him.

After hearing what Wang Sheng said, the monk told Wang Sheng that the monster he saw earlier was called the "Ghost with Painted Skin." She was originally a woman from a normal household, but her husband had a change of heart, and she died of depression. After her death, she became an evil demon who specifically targeted married men. After the man changed his heart and abandoned his wife, she would tear open the man's chest and eat his heart.

Wang Sheng begged him to save his life. The monk gave Wang Sheng a Taoist talisman and told him to hang the talisman on the door of the bedroom, and that would chase the Ghost with Painted Skin away.

At night, Wang Sheng hid in the bedroom and did not dare to sleep. Suddenly, he heard footsteps from the outside. The sound of the footsteps was circling by the door.

他偷偷地透过门缝向外看，见那个女子惧怕符咒的法力不敢靠近。她徘徊了很久，最终离去。

He secretly peeked outside from the small door crack and saw that the woman was extremely afraid of the magic power of the talisman and did not dare to get near. She wandered for a long time, then eventually walked away.

只是没想到，她刚刚离开，平静的夜晚突然刮起了大风，风吹掉了门口的符咒。还没等王生反应过来，那女人就冲进卧室，一把撕开王生的胸膛，挖出心脏后就带着心脏离开了。

Unexpectedly, as soon as she left, a gust of big wind suddenly blew by in the silent night and blew away the talisman on the door. Before Wang Sheng had a chance to react, that woman rushed into the bedroom, tore open Wang Sheng's chest, and dug out his heart. Then she left with the heart.

本故事改编自《聊斋志异》里的短篇故事《画皮》，作者：蒲松龄，生卒年代：公元1610年-1715年。原故事较长，后面还有道士如何杀掉女鬼，王生的妻子如何救王生的情节。

This story is an adaptation of the short story "Painted Skin" from *Strange Tales from a Chinese Studio*. Author: Pu Songling, 1610-1715. The original story was lengthy and included plots such as how the Taoist monk killed the female demon and how Wang Sheng's wife rescued Wang Sheng.

本页插图选自《聊斋全图》第八册，清光绪时期绘本，现藏于奥地利国家图书馆。

【画皮 huà pí】

字面含义是：在人皮上画画。《画皮》是中国著名的鬼故事，又名《画皮鬼》或者《鬼画皮》。它是清代小说家蒲松龄创作的短篇小说集《聊斋志异》中的一篇作品。该故事情节曲折，文笔生动，形象逼真。在现代中国，这一故事被翻拍成各种影视剧作品，使得该故事情节更为家喻户晓。

The literal translation is painting on human skin. "The Painted Skin" is a famous ghost story in China. It is also known as "The Ghost with Painted Skin" or "Demon Paints Skin." It is a piece from the short novel collection Strange Tales from a Chinese Studio by the Qing dynasty novelist Pu Songling. The story has plot twists and turns, with vivid descriptions and realistic imagery. In modern China, this story has been adapted into various films and television productions, making the story plot well known in every household.

【包袱 bāo fu】

古代时没有现代的包或者行李箱，人们出行时若是想要带一些衣服和生活用品，就用一块布把要带的衣服包裹起来，然后把布的两头系在身上。这样就制作出了一个临时的包儿，人们把这个包儿就叫做包袱。

在现代，人们当然已经不用这样的包袱来装自己的衣物。但是包袱这个词的另外的含义仍然被广泛使用，那就是：负担。比如："你不要有心理包袱，只要认真做了，结果怎么样不重要。"这里的"心理包袱"意思就是"心理负担"。

画中人物右手拿的就是一个包袱 ➡

本插图选自《清末各样人物图册》，绘于1770 - 1790年，现藏于荷兰国立世界文化博物馆。

In ancient society, there were no modern bags or suitcases. When people were traveling and wanted to bring some clothes and daily necessities with them, they would use a piece of fabric to wrap all the clothes they wanted to bring, and then tie the two ends of the fabric around their body. This way they created a temporary makeshift bag, which people called this kind of bag "bao fu."

In modern society, obviously, people no longer use this kind of "bao fu" to pack their clothes. However the other meaning of the the word "bao fu" is still widely used, and the meaning is "burden." For example: Don't carry any bao fu in your heart. As long as you do it earnestly, then the result is not as important. In this sentence, the "bao fu in your heart" is referring to a "mental burden."

【正妻 zhèng qī】 【小妾 xiǎo qiè】

在中国封建社会，实行一夫多妻制。即，一个男人可以迎娶多名女人做自己的妻子。由于封建等级制度，男人会选择来自上等阶层的女人做自己的正妻。如果男人来自中下等阶层，也娶不到上等阶层的女人，那么他通常会选择第一个嫁给自己的女人做正妻。除了正妻，其他的老婆都叫做小妾。正妻和小妾之间也是有阶级制度的，如果正妻觉得小妾做错了什么事，是可以惩罚小妾的。

因此，我们在形容皇帝或者封建社会的其他官员和富人的时候，经常会用"三妻四妾"，"三妻六妾"，"妻妾成群"这样的词来表示这个人有很多妻子。

In China's feudal society, polygamous marriage was permitted. As in, a man could marry multiple women as his wives. Due to the feudal hierarchy, a man would choose a woman from the higher class as his legal/official wife. If a man was from the middle or lower class, then he wouldn't be able to marry a woman from the higher class. In that case, he would normally choose the first woman who married him as his legal first wife. Apart from his legal first wife, all his other wives were called concubines. There was a hierarchy between the first wife and concubines as well. If the first wife believed that the concubine did something wrong, then she could punish the concubine.

Therefore, when we describe the emperor or other governors and wealthy men in a feudal society, we often use expressions such as "three wives four concubines," "three wives six concubines" or "a group of wives and concubines" to describe that this person has many wives.

【知书达礼 zhī shū dá lǐ】

知书达礼，或者知书达理。是用来赞扬封建社会里的一些女性的词汇。字面含义就是："认识汉字，可以阅读书籍，并且知道各种礼仪。"在中国封建社会，女人不能去学校上学。所以，只有官员和富人家才有钱去请老师来家里教女儿识字，读书。通常情况下，会教一些诗歌，和有关礼仪的书籍。所以知书达礼就变成了赞扬女人可以看得懂书，行为得体的词汇。

在现代中国，无论男孩还是女孩都必须接受教育。中国的义务教育制度一共是9年，这九年期间，如果父母不让小孩去上学，这是违法的事情。所以，现在也没有人会用知书达礼这个词去赞扬女人了。

知书达礼 or 知书达理, it is a word used to praise some women in a feudal society. The literal translation is "knowing Chinese characters, can read, and also know all kinds of etiquettes." In China's feudal society, women couldn't go to school to study. Therefore, only officials or wealthy families had money to hire teachers to go to their homes to teach their daughters characters and read. Normally, the teacher would teach poems and some books related to etiquette. As a result, 知书达礼 became a word that praised women who could read and had well-mannered etiquette.

In modern China, whether they are boys or girls, they must receive an education. China's mandatory education is 9 years in total. In these nine years, it is against the law if parents forbid their children to go to school. Therefore, nowadays no one uses 知书达礼 to praise a woman anymore.

本插图选自《丽姝萃秀图》，
清代赫达资绘，
现藏于台北故宫博物院。

【楚楚可怜 chǔ chǔ kě lián】

楚楚可怜是一个成语。"楚楚"本来是用来形容植物刚长出来的叶子，非常柔软，脆弱。"可怜"在古代中文里是可爱的意思。后来，楚楚可怜经常用来形容女子瘦小，妩媚，娇柔。也用来形容词女子的表情，看起来很悲伤，令人感觉到可怜和心疼。

楚楚可怜 is an idiom. 楚楚 was originally used to describe newly sprouted leaves, which are soft and fragile. 可怜 in ancient Chinese meant cute. Later on, 楚楚可怜 is often used to describe women who are slim, charming, and gentle. It is also used to describe a woman's facial expression that looks so sad that one's heart breaks for her and pities her.

【春心萌动 chūn xīn méng dòng】

"春"指的是春天，是植物重新发芽，生长，天气也变得温暖的季节。 人们认为春天是美好的季节，看到春天的景色心情会变得激动，而这种激动的心情和男女之间互相爱慕的心情是差不多的。所以，人们会用"春"来描述男女之间的感情。

比如故事中的"春心萌动"指的是王生对女子动了情，心跳加速。还有"春心荡漾"，指的是一个人非常喜欢另一个人，他的心情像是水里的浪花，一直在荡漾，无法平静。还有"思春"指的是希望找个人谈恋爱，对异性有渴望的情绪。当然"春"也可以单纯指代春天，不一定都是指男女之间的爱慕之情，例如"春暖花开"，"满园春色"，"春意阑珊"，"春色撩人" 等都是用来形容春天美景的词汇。

春 refers to spring, a season where plants sprout anew, and grow, and the weather becomes warm. People believe that spring is a wonderful season. Seeing the scenery in spring stirs excitement. This feeling of excitement is similar to mutual romantic affection between men and women. Therefore, people use 春 to describe the feelings between men and women.

For example, in the story, 春心萌动 shows that Wang Sheng developed feelings for the woman, and his heartbeat increased. In addition, 春心荡漾 is an expression used to describe liking someone so much that his feelings are like the waves in the water, always rippling, and can't calm down. The word 思春 means the strong desire for the opposite gender and wanting to fall in love. Of course, 春 can also simply mean spring without any indication of romantic affection between a man and a woman. For example, 春暖花开, 满园春色, 春意阑珊, 春色撩人 are all expressions used to describe the beautiful scenery in spring.

【一夜缠绵 yí yè chán mián】

"缠绵"指的是像线一样缠到一起，没有办法分开。用来形容男女之间的亲密接触。那么一夜缠绵指的就是男人和女人整个晚上缠在一起的意思。

缠绵 means tangled together like threads that can't be separated. It is used to describe the intimate touch between a man and a woman. So 一夜缠绵 means the man and woman spent the entire night tangled together (Translator's Note: a euphemism to say that they had sex that night).

【云雨 yún yǔ】

在中国古代，由于受到封建思维的影响以及中国人对道德和礼仪的高度重视，人们从来不会在文学作品中直白地说"做爱"，而是习惯用更隐晦的方法去讲述。其中"云雨"就是一个常见的"做爱"两字的代名词。

In ancient China, due to the influence of feudal thinking and the high emphasis that Chinese people placed on morality and etiquette, people would never explicitly mention "to have sex" in literary works. Instead, it was customary to allude to it indirectly. Among them, 云雨 is a commonly used word to express "to have sex."

那为什么"云雨"可以表示那样的含义呢？据记载，在战国时期，楚国有一位王，人们叫他为楚怀王。有一天，楚怀王到一个地方去游玩，玩得累了，就睡着了。梦里一位自称来自巫山的美人主动要求和他发生了性关系，美人离开时说自己住在一个"朝云暮雨"的地方，意思就是早上有云，晚上下雨的地方。楚怀王醒后难以忘记梦里的美好经历，他派人去巫山寻找这样的地方，但却没有找到。从那以后"云雨"或者"巫山云雨"就成为了"做爱"的文雅说法，这种说法不仅没那么直白，还很有浪漫色彩。

Why can 云雨 be used to express that meaning? According to the records, in the Warring States period (Translator's Note: the Warring States period was an era in Chinese history between 770 BC and 221 BC), the State of Chu had a king, people called him King Huai of Chu. One day, King Huai of Chu traveled to a place. When he got tired, he fell asleep. He dreamt of a beautiful woman from Mountain Wu who offered to have sex with him. Before the beautiful woman left, she said she lived in a place that is 朝云暮雨, meaning it was a place where there were clouds in the morning and rained at night. After King Huai of Chu woke up, he couldn't forget the wonderful experience in his dream. He sent people to Mountain Wu to look for this place, but they couldn't find it. Since then, 云雨 or 巫山云雨 became an elegant expression for "to have sex." This expression is less explicit and even somewhat romantic.

随着时代的变迁，在现代中国，大家也不再用"云雨"一词来指代"做爱"了。不过直接说"做爱"对于中国人来说也仍然有些害羞和尴尬。

With the changing times, in modern China, people no longer use the expression 云雨 to refer to "having sex." But saying the phrase "have sex" directly still remains somewhat shy and embarrassing for Chinese people.

Generated by AI Image Gen

【道士 dào shi】 【道观 dào guàn】

道教是发源于中国，由中国人创立的宗教。所以也被称为"本土宗教"。它大概于公元2世纪形成，现在已有1700多年的历史。道士指的是道教的神职人员，相当于佛教里的和尚，基督教里的神父。人们普遍认为道士可以驱邪驱鬼。道观就是道士们进行修炼的地方。在中国佛教和道教都是很流行的宗教，一般叫做"某某寺"的地方指的是佛寺，而一般叫做"某某观"，"某某庙"的地方才是道观。

Taoism originated in China and was established by the Chinese. Therefore, it is also known as the "local religion." It is estimated to have formed around the 2nd century, with a history of 1700 years. 道士 refers to the clergy in Taoism, like the monks in Buddhism or the priests in Christianity. People commonly believed that 道士 could exorcise evil spirits. 道观 are places where Taoists cultivate (engage in their spiritual practices). In China, both Buddhism and Taoism are popular religions. Normally a place called "something 寺 sì" is a Buddhist temple, while "something 观 guān" or "something 庙 miào" is a Taoist Temple.

← 清代末年的一位道士

本插图选自《清末各样人物图册》，现藏于荷兰国立世界文化博物馆。

在中华人民共和国成立后，政府倡导宗教自由，允许人们有自己的宗教信仰，无论是基督教，佛教，道教还是伊斯兰教。但是在学校里，教科书上，和官方媒体中，政府还是更大力地倡导人们摆脱封建思维，相信科学，而非宗教。所以现今很多中国人，尤其是在学校接受过教育的人们都没有宗教信仰。只是无论是佛教还是道教在中国的历史上都存在了上千年，它们对中国人的文化，节日习俗，生活习惯和观念仍然有着不可磨灭的影响。

Since the founding of the People's Republic of China, the government advocated freedom of religion, allowing people to have their own religious beliefs, whether it is Christianity, Buddhism, Taoism, or Islam. But in school, textbooks, and government media, the government heavily promotes and encourages people to break free from feudalistic thinking, and encourages people to believe in science instead of religious beliefs. Consequently, many Chinese citizens, particularly those who have received education don't have a religion. Nevertheless, both Buddhism and Taoism have been around in China for thousands of years, leaving an indelible mark on Chinese culture, festival customs, lifestyle habits, and beliefs.

◄ 位于成都青城山的
一所道观

【法力 fǎ lì】

最开始指的是佛教和道教中，和尚或者道士除魔降妖的能力。现在指所有超出正常人的能力的超能力。

Originally referred to the ability of monks or Taoist priests in Buddhism and Taoism to exorcise demons and vanquish monsters. Now it refers to abilities or superpowers that exceed those of ordinary people.

【符咒 fú zhòu】

道士在纸上写咒语，用于作法，也就是施展他的法力，比如驱除鬼怪，召唤风雨等。

Taoist monks inscribe incantations on paper for rituals to utilize their magical power to ward off evil spirits, exorcise ghosts or demons, summon the wind or the rain, etc.

【邪气 xié qì】

邪气在本故事里指的是妖怪或者鬼散发出来的气息。此外，邪气也可以指不正当的风气或者行为。有一句古话是："君子行正气，小人行邪气。"意思就是品德高尚的人散发着一身正气，而道德败坏的人则是一身邪气。

邪气 in this story refers to the aura emitted by demons or ghosts. In addition, 邪气 can also refer to improper customs or behaviors. There is an ancient saying that goes "君子行正气，小人行邪气。" (Note: a noble person carries righteous energy, a petty person carries evil energy) which means a person of high moral character emits a virtuous aura, whereas those with morally corrupt behavior exude an evil aura.

【梳妆 shū zhuāng】

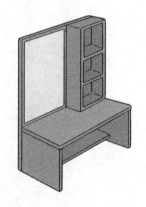

梳妆的"梳"指的是梳头，"妆"指的是化妆。在中国古代，女子都留很长的头发，梳妆要花比较长的时间。现代女子不太会像古代女人一样留那么长的头发，所以也不太用梳妆这个词，而是会用"化妆"。但是仍然会使用"梳妆台"这个词，它指的是放女性化妆用品等，并且通常都带有镜子的一种家具。

In the word 梳妆, 梳 refers to combing one's hair while 妆 refers to putting on makeup. In ancient China, women had really long hair, so 梳妆 (styling their hair and putting on makeup) took a long time. Modern women don't really keep their hair as long as the ancient women. Consequently, the word 梳妆 is not really used. Instead, they will use the word 化妆 (put on makeup). However, we still use the word 梳妆台 (vanity table) which is a piece of furniture that is used to store women's cosmetic products and such, and often comes with a mirror.

吴绛仙

▲正在对镜梳妆描眉的女子

本插图选自《古代美人图》，清末 周培春 绘，现藏于圣彼得堡国立大学图书馆。

无头鬼

The Headless Ghost

本页插图选自《聊斋全图》第六十册，清光绪时期绘本，现藏于奥地利国家图书馆。

27

在清代有个小县城，该县城具体在哪里，叫什么名字已经无人知晓。但这县城里有两个人，一个姓金，一个姓李，他们俩讲了一个自己亲身经历的故事，这故事十分精彩，一直流传到今天。

话说有这么一天晚上，李某睡觉前去上厕所。厕所在院子的外面，一条路的旁边。他上完厕所后，正准备回房间时，隐约看到一个老人提着个酒壶在路上行走。这倒是没什么好奇怪的，只是老人后面的不远处还跟着一个壮汉，看起来鬼鬼祟祟的。

李某感到很好奇，就躲在一棵大树后面，想看看这个壮汉要干什么。老人这时听到了后面的脚步声，回头一看，看见后面的人只长了半张脸。那半张脸上有一只眼睛，半个鼻子和半张嘴。老人吓得大叫了一声。那半脸鬼张开嘴巴，他的牙齿居然是完整的，一半长在脸上，一半悬在空中。老人转身就跑，壮汉紧追不舍，老人脚下一滑，摔倒在地！

壮汉来到老人身边，伸手去扶他。老人转过身来，就在这瞬间，壮汉发现这老人的脑袋不见了！脖子上面一片黑色，鼻子嘴巴什么都没有！

During the Qing Dynasty, there was a small town. The precise location of said town or what the town was called, is no longer known. But in the said town, there were two people, one's last name was Jin, and the other one was Li. They told a captivating story from their own experiences that has been passed down to the present day.

It was said that there was this one night, Mr. Li was going to the restroom before bed. The restroom was outside the courtyard, on the side of a road. After going to the restroom, he was about to head back to his room. But then he caught a glimpse of an old man carrying a jug of liquor walking on the road. That itself wasn't strange, but it was that not too far behind the old man, there was a burly man following him, looking suspicious.

Mr. Li was curious. He hid behind a big tree. He wanted to see what the burly man wanted to do. Right then the old man heard footsteps from behind. He turned around and saw that the person behind him only had half of a face. There was only one eye on the half face, half of a nose, and half of a mouth. The old man was so scared that he let out a scream. The half-faced ghost opened its mouth, showing a full set of teeth surprisingly. Half of the teeth were on the face, the other half were floating in the air. The old man turned around and started running. The burly man followed tightly. The old man slipped and fell onto the ground!

The burly man got up next to the old man and extended his hand to help him. The old man turned around, and right at that moment, the burly man noticed that the old man no longer had a head! It was pitch black from his neck and above. There was no nose or mouth!

这回轮到壮汉大叫起来："妈呀！有鬼！有鬼！"声音凄厉，令人毛骨悚然。

李某离得有些远，看得不是很清楚，他正在纳闷怎么两个人都叫有鬼呢？忽然，不知道从哪冒出一个穿白色衣服的人。他年纪不大，看起来文质彬彬，很有教养。这白衣男子来到两人身边，笑呵呵地说："我怎么没看见鬼？我只看到了一壶酒。月色这么好，咱们能相聚也是缘分。我这还有一些下酒菜，咱们一起喝一杯吧！"

壮汉和老人还惊魂未定，被白衣男子硬是拉着坐在路边。白衣男子拿起酒壶喝了一口酒，然后把酒壶递给壮汉，让壮汉也喝一口。壮汉接过酒壶，正不知该怎么办好，只见白衣男子把自己的脑袋摘了下来，放到膝盖上，那颗头上的眼睛看看老人，又看看壮汉，嘴巴还继续笑着说："喝呀！怎么不喝呢？"

老人和壮汉一言不发，好像是被吓傻了。白衣男看他们俩发呆的眼神，生气地说："你们盯着我干嘛？我长得很奇怪吗？你们等着，我去叫我师父来，他的模样才叫奇怪呢！"说完，就把脑袋

This time it was the burly man's turn to scream: "Oh my goodness! There is a ghost! There is a ghost!" The sound was piercing, sending shivers down one's spine.

Mr. Li was kind of far away, so he couldn't see it clearly. Right when he was wondering why these two people both screamed there was a ghost, suddenly, a person wearing white clothes appeared out of the blue. He was quite young and seemed courteous, elegant, and well-mannered. The man dressed in white got up next to these two people and said while smiling, "Why don't I see any ghosts? I only see a jug of liquor. The moonlight is beautiful. We seem to have quite a fate to gather together. I have some snacks to go with the drink. Let's have a drink!"

The burly man and the old man were still unsettled from what just happened but the man in white insisted and sat them down to the side of the road. The man in white took the liquor jug and had a sip, then he handed the liquor jug to the burly man, to have him take a sip. The burly man took the liquor jug, unsure what to do. And right then he saw the man in white take down his own head and set it on his knees. The eyes on the head looked at the old man, then the burly man, its mouth continued to smile and said, "Drink! Why are you not drinking?"

The old man and the burly man said not a single word, seemingly petrified. The man in white looked at their dazed gaze, and angrily said, "Why are you staring at me? Do I look weird? You guys wait. I will go bring my master. His appearance is truly weird!" As soon as he finished speaking,

放在地上，无头的身子飞奔而去。留下两个人呆在原地。那颗头还在不停地讲话，表达自己的不满。

不一会儿，无头的身子又跑了回来，后面还跟着另一个怪物。这怪物的身体和正常人一样，只是长着九颗人头。九张嘴同时在讲话，叽叽喳喳，吵个不停，根本听不清在说些什么。

那颗摆在地上的脑袋得意地说："你们看！我师父长得比我更奇怪吧！"老人和壮汉身体一软，纷纷瘫倒在地。

正在大树后面偷看的李某也被吓得魂不附体。他拔腿想跑，却踢到了什么软绵绵的东西，把他给绊倒了。他定睛一看，地上慢慢升起了两只没穿鞋的脚掌。两只脚像植物发芽一样，向上生长，一会儿又长出了小腿，大腿，身子，肩膀，头部。一个完整的人形怪物倒插在地上，对着李某伸出了手。李某赶紧爬起来没命地狂奔到旁边金某的家里。

金某听了李某的叙述，点燃两个火把，又跑回大树旁。他们拿着火把去烧那倒立的鬼，鬼吓坏了，赶紧又钻回地里。他们又拿着火把去追那只九头鬼，九头鬼

he put his head on the ground. Then the headless body dashed off, leaving the two of them dumbfounded at the same spot. That head was still talking nonstop, expressing his dissatisfaction.

Shortly after, the headless body ran back, followed by another monster. The monster's body was the same as a normal human's, except it had nine heads. Nine mouths were talking at the same, chatting and arguing nonstop. It was impossible to hear clearly what they were saying.

That head on the ground said with pride, "See! My master looks a lot more strange than me!" The old man and the burly man both went limp, passed out on the ground one after another.

Mr. Li, who had been watching secretly behind the tree was also scared out of his wits. He was about to bolt off, but he kicked something soft and squishy, causing him to stumble and fall. He took a closer look. Two feet not wearing any shoes slowly rose from the ground. The two feet rose like a plant, sprouting upwards. Shortly it grew legs, thighs, torso, shoulders, and a head. One complete human-shaped monster appeared upside down on the ground, extending its hand toward Mr. Li. Mr. Li quickly scrambled to his feet and sprinted for dear life to the nearby Mr. Jin's house.

Upon hearing Mr. Li's description, Mr. Jin lit up two torches and ran back to the tree. Holding the torches, they approached the upside-down ghost to burn it. The ghost was scared, and quickly burrowed back into the ground. They chased the nine-headed

吓得哇哇直叫，变成一只九头鸟飞到天上逃走了。白衣鬼慌忙地四处寻找自己放在地上的脑袋，好不容易找到后，把脑袋安到脖子上，慌不择路地跑了。

地上就只剩下那老人和壮汉。金某和李某叫醒了他们俩。原来，壮汉先是在朋友家玩游戏喝酒，因为游戏输了，朋友们开玩笑用墨水涂黑了他半张脸。壮汉想着天黑也没人看见，就计划回家再洗脸。但是在回家的路上他看到老人带着一壶酒，想要跟老人讨一口酒喝，就跟在老人的后面，没想到吓坏了老人。老人慌乱中摔倒在地，脸朝下摔进了一个黑土堆里，脸上沾满了黑灰，在晚上看起来就好像是脑袋不见了。这两个人疑神疑鬼，互相怀疑对方是无头鬼，不料真正的鬼还在后面呢！

本故事改编自清代作家黄钧宰(生卒年代：1826年-1895年)的短篇小说。

ghost with the torches. The nine-headed ghost got scared, screamed in terror, transformed into a nine-headed bird, and flew away. The man in white frantically searched for his head on the ground. Finally finding it after some struggle, he attached his head to his neck and ran away in a panic without a clear direction.

Only the old man and the burly man remained on the ground. Mr. Jin and Mr. Li woke them up. Turned out that the burly man was playing games and drinking at his friend's house. Because he lost the game, his friends teased him by painting half of his face black using black ink. The burly man thought since it was dark, no one would see him, so he planned to go home and then wash his face. But on the way back home, he saw the old man carrying a jug of liquor. He wanted to ask for a drink. He followed behind the old man but unexpectedly scared the old man. The old man fell onto the ground in a panic, and he face-planted a big puddle of black dirt, which got all over his face. At night, it looked as if the old man had lost his head. These two people were very suspicious. They suspected the other person was a headless ghost. Little did they know, the real ghosts were behind them.

This story was an adaptation of a short story by Huang Junzai (1826-1895), an author during the Qing Dynasty.

【李某 lǐ mǒu】

"某"代替没有明确指出的时间，地点，人物，事件等。比如，某天，某人，某事。在故事里，我们只知道这个人姓李，不知道他的名字，所以我们就称他为李某。

某 substitutes unspecified details such as time, place, person, events, etc. For example, a certain day, a certain person, or a certain matter. In the story, we only know that this person's last name is Li. We don't know his first name, so we refer to him as Li Mou or Mr. Li.

【鬼鬼祟祟 guǐ guǐ suì suì】

"祟"原本指的也是鬼的意思。古代人相信鬼的存在，他们一般认为鬼不能在白天出现，鬼要借着人的身体才能做出一些活动。所以像鬼一样，就表示这个人不能光明正大地行动。那么，鬼鬼祟祟就用来形容一些偷偷摸摸，不光明正大的行为。

祟 (suì) also means ghost. People in ancient society believed in the existence of ghosts. They generally believed that ghosts couldn't appear during the day. Ghosts needed to use a human body to carry out activities. So "like a ghost" means that this person can't act openly and honestly. Therefore, the term 鬼鬼祟祟 is used to describe some sneaky and underhanded behaviors or actions.

【毛骨悚然 máo gǔ sǒng rán】

毛骨悚然是一个成语。其中，"毛"指的是毛发；"骨"指的是骨头；"悚然"是害怕的意思。人在害怕的时候，头发和汗毛会竖起来，骨头甚至都觉得冷。所以毛骨悚然就用来形容非常害怕，非常恐惧。

毛骨悚然 is a Chinese idiom. In the phrase, 毛 means hair. 骨 means bone. 悚然 means scared. When a person is scared, their hair stands up (having goosebumps), and even their bones feel cold. Therefore, 毛骨悚然 is used to describe when one is very scared or frightened.

【文质彬彬 wén zhì bīn bīn】

文质彬彬是一个成语。"文"指的是文采，就是写作的能力与风格；"质"指的是人的品质；"彬彬"的意思是文雅，得体。所以文质彬彬是用来形容某个人看起来受过教育，有礼貌，举止文雅。

文质彬彬 is a Chinese idiom. 文 means literary talent, as in writing ability and style. 质 means a person's quality. 彬彬 means elegant and courteous. Therefore 文质彬彬 is used to describe a person who is educated, polite, courteous, and elegant.

【惊魂未定 jīng hún wèi dìng】 【魂不附体 hún bú fù tǐ】

惊魂未定里的"魂"指的是灵魂。中国古代人认为，灵魂或者魂魄是人身体里的一种看不见的，非物质的东西。灵魂如果离开了人的身体后，人就会死亡。所以就有很多带"魂"字的成语。尤其是在讲人被惊吓的情况，会经常用到"魂"字。比如，惊魂未定：魂魄都受到了惊吓，还没有平静下来。魂不附体：被吓得灵魂好像都快脱离身体了，也就是快被吓死了。

The 魂 in 惊魂未定 is referring to one's spirit/soul. The ancient Chinese believed that spirits or souls are invisible, non-matter substances that are in one's body. If the spirit/soul leaves one's body, then the person dies. As a result, there are many idioms with the character 魂. For example, 惊魂未定 means even the spirit/soul has been frightened and hasn't calmed down. 魂不附体 means one gets so scared as if the spirit/soul is leaving one's body, as in scared to death.

【慌不择路 huāng bù zé lù】

慌不择路是一个成语。它的含义很好理解：过于**慌**乱而在逃走的时候**不**能选**择**一条好走的**路**。意思就是非常慌乱地逃走了。

慌不择路 is a Chinese idiom. Its meaning is relatively easy to understand. When one is overly panicky and can't choose a good path to escape. In other words, escaping while panicking.

古代画册中所画的一个慌不择路的男人➡

本插图选自《聊斋全图》第四十七册，
现藏于奥地利国家图书馆。

【疑神疑鬼 yí shén yí guǐ】

疑神疑鬼是一个成语。字面的意思是：一会儿怀疑那是神仙，一会儿怀疑那是鬼怪。形容某个人神经过敏，没有根据地胡乱猜想。

疑神疑鬼 is a Chinese idiom. The surface meaning is one second suspecting it is a god, the next second suspecting it is a ghost. It is used to describe a person who is mentally unstable or nervous and thus comes up with nonsense illogically.

旱魃鬼

Hanba the Drought Demon

本插图由AI Image Gen生成

19世纪下半叶，以英，法为首的西方列强向中国先后发动多次战争。战败的清政府被迫签订了许多不平等条约。中国逐渐沦为半封建半殖民主义国家。然而，雪上加霜的是：在这本就风雨飘摇的中华大地上自然灾祸也不断。我们今天的故事就发生在这个时期的山东济南。

济南的夏天本应是多雨的季节。但这一年，从春天开始就一滴雨都没有降过。4个月过去了，附近的河流早已干涸，遍布全城大大小小的上百个泉眼也不再涌动。田地里，一排排干枯的农作物像是一个个骷髅，立在龟裂的大地上。

当地人认为这场大旱是旱魃鬼在作怪。旱魃鬼是传说中能够引发旱灾的鬼。据说，人死了若是对这个世界还有留恋不愿离去，他的尸体就有可能在死后一百天的时候变成旱魃鬼。变成旱魃后，他的尸体不会腐烂，他的坟上还会往外渗水，那水是绿色的，映得整个坟丘也是一片绿色。只有烧毁旱魃鬼的尸体，才能降服旱魃鬼，之后，天才会下雨。

In the second half of the 19th century, Western powers led by Great Britain and France launched multiple wars against China. The defeated Qing Dynasty government was forced to sign many unequal treaties. China gradually became a semi-feudal and semi-colonial country. However, to make matters worse, natural disasters continued to afflict the already tumultuous Chinese land. Our story today unfolds during this period in Jinan, a city in the Shandong province.

The summer in Jinan was supposed to be a rainy season. However this one year, there had not been a single rain drop since the start of spring. Four months had passed, and the nearby streams had already dried up. The hundreds of small and big springheads throughout the entire city had stopped flowing. In the fields, rows and rows of dried crops were like skeletons, standing on the cracked land.

The locals believed that this drought was a result of the Drought Demon, Hanba. According to the legend, Hanba is a demon that can cause droughts. It is said that when a person dies, and they still have lingering feelings and are not willing to leave. Then, their corpse has a chance of turning into Hanba (Drought Demon) after 100 days. After becoming a Hanba, their body will not rot. Their grave will leak water, and the water will be green, painting the entire grave green. Only burning and destroying Hanba's corpse will conquer Hanba. After that, rain will fall from the sky.

只是这一次，人们寻遍了各家的坟墓，也没发现旱魃鬼的踪迹。正在一筹莫展之时，一个叫做李大的外地人来济南办事。因为没有充足的盘缠，李大找到了城郊的一个破败的佛寺，准备在那里住上几晚。

这佛寺过于破旧，夜晚凉风习习，李大只好钻进一个破了的大鼓里，这才得以入睡。睡到半夜，他被一阵喧闹声音吵醒。他从鼓里探出头来，看见有十几个人在院子里。原来，他们是一伙强盗，刚抢了当地一户富人家，躲到这里来分东西。

其中一些人拿到了自己的那一份东西就纷纷离去。最后只剩下两个人留在那里继续分东西。李大不敢出声，仍然藏在大鼓里。突然，一个人抽出刀来，一刀砍死同伴，卷走所有的东西，离开了佛寺。

李大十分吃惊，不知道怎么办才好，一阵冷风刮进院子里。一个黑影一蹦一跳地来到院中，它的身形很像是人类，但是蹦跳的动作却像是一只巨大的猴子，而且它浑身长满绿毛，两只眼睛也冒着瘆人的绿光。

But this time, people searched every single grave, and couldn't find sight of Hanba. After not having any leads, a non-local called Li Da came to Jinan to take care of some things. Because he didn't have enough money, he found a dilapidated Buddhist temple on the outskirts of the city, planning on staying there for a few nights.

The Buddhist temple was extremely old and dilapidated. At night there were cold winds. Li Da had to crawl into a broken drum to sleep. Around midnight, he was awakened by a commotion. He peeked out from the drum and saw more than ten people in the courtyard. Turned out, they were robbers. They just robbed a local wealthy family and came here to divide up the loot.

Some of the people took their portions and left one after another. Leaving only two people there to continue dividing the loot up. Li Da didn't dare to make any noise and stayed hidden in the big drum. Suddenly, one of them took out a knife and killed his partner in one stab. He wrapped up everything and left the temple.

Li Da was very shocked. He wasn't sure what to do. Then a gust of cold wind blew into the courtyard. A black shadow hopped into the courtyard. Its shape resembled very much like that of a human. But the hopping movement resembled that of a giant ape. And its entire body had green fur grown on it. Its two eyes flashed eerie green light.

这绿毛怪物看到院子的尸体，低头闻了闻，拍着巴掌咯咯地笑了起来，笑声像是猫头鹰的怪叫。然后，它迅速把尸体撕成一块一块的，放进嘴里大吃起来，咀嚼骨头的清脆声音响彻佛寺。吃完后，怪物就跳进了佛寺的后院，不知躲进了什么地方。李大赶忙从鼓中跳出来，一路狂奔，逃离了佛寺。

李大一直向城里跑去，也不知道目的地是哪里，就只疯了一般地逃命。结果撞到了搜城的衙役，被抓了起来。原来富人家遭抢后，马上报了官，县令命手下立刻搜寻强盗，就抓到了在夜里狂奔的李大。

李大向县令详细描述了他在佛寺里看到的情况。县令按照李大提供的线索抓住了强盗们，但却没有找到那只绿毛鬼。

听李大的描述，这绿毛鬼分明就是引发旱灾的旱魃鬼。只是要怎么样才能抓到它呢？正在束手无策之时，一位叫做陆锟的武林高手正巧路过济南，听说此事就自告奋勇前来帮忙。

The green-furred monster saw the corpses in the courtyard, lowered its head, sniffed, then clapped its hands and started laughing. Its laugh sounded like the strange hoot of an owl. Then, it quickly tore up the corpses into pieces, put them into his mouth, and started devouring them with relish. The crisp sound of bone crunching echoed throughout the Buddhist temple. After it finished eating, the monster hopped into the backyard of the Buddhist temple and hid in some unknown place. Li Da quickly jumped out of the drum, ran like crazy, and escaped the Buddhist temple.

Li Da kept running toward the inner city. He wasn't sure where his destination was. He just ran like crazy to save his life. He ended up colliding with the police officers searching the city and was detained. Turned out the wealthy family reported to the authorities soon after they were robbed. The county magistrate ordered his subordinates to immediately start searching for the robbers. Then they caught Li Da, who was running wild at night.

Li Da described in detail what he saw at the Buddhist temple to the county magistrate. The county magistrate caught the robbers based on the lead provided by Li Da. However, they didn't find that green-furred demon.

After hearing Li Da's description, it was clear that the green-furred demon was Hanba, the Drought Demon that caused the drought. But how could they catch it? As they were feeling helpless, a highly skilled martial artist named Lu Kun was passing through Jinan. He offered to help after hearing this incident.

夜幕降临后，他来到佛寺，四处搜寻都没发现旱魃鬼。他想起李大的描述，就装作死人躺在地上。不一会儿，一阵寒风袭来，那怪物已经来到陆锟的面前。陆锟用刀猛刺旱魃鬼的腿，但却像砍到石头一样。他正想用力再砍，刀已被旱魃抢去，扔到一旁。陆锟逃到佛像的后面，旱魃鬼追过来打碎了佛像。眼看陆锟就要成为旱魃鬼的口中之物，一条巨蛇突然出现，把怪物紧紧缠住。陆锟捡起地上的刀，用力向旱魃的肚皮刺去，旱魃大叫一声瘫倒在地。

旱魃倒地后，那条神秘的大蛇又游走了。陆锟把旱魃挪到院子里，点燃了一把火，之后把旱魃扔到火里焚烧。原本红色的火苗立刻变成了绿色，照亮了周边几里地远的地方。

当天夜里就天降甘霖，雨水湿润了大地，填满了河流，那持续足有5个月的旱灾就这样结束了。

本故事改编自清代作家王韬所著的《淞隐漫录》中的一篇小说。原著发表于1885年。

After nightfall, he came to the Buddhist temple. He searched everywhere but couldn't find Hanba at all. Then he remembered Li Da's description, so he pretended to be dead and lay on the ground. Shortly after, a gust of chill wind swept in. The monster had already arrived in front of Lu Kun. Lu Kun used his sword and stabbed fiercely into Hanba's leg, but it felt as if it just stabbed a rock. As he was thinking about stabbing it again, Hanba had already taken the sword and thrown it to the side. Li Kun ran behind the Budda statue. Hanba ran after him and broke the Budda statue. As Lu Kun was about to become Hanba's meal, a giant snake suddenly appeared, coiling the monster tightly. Lu Kun picked up the sword on the ground, aimed at Hanba's stomach, and stabbed with force. Hanba let out a scream and collapsed onto the ground.

After Hanba collapsed onto the ground, that mysterious snake had also slithered away. Lu Kun moved Hanba to the courtyard, lit up a fire, and threw Hanba into the fire to burn. The original red flames immediately turned green, illuminating the surroundings several kilometers away.

That very night, sweet rain fell from the sky, moistening the earth and filling up the rivers. The drought that had persisted for a full five months came to an end.

This story was an adaptation of a short story from the book *Jottings from Carefree Travel* by the Qing Dynasty author Wang Tao. Originally published in 1885.

【旱魃 hàn bá】

旱魃，又称旱魃鬼，是中国古代神话传说中引起旱灾的怪物。关于旱魃的文字记载最早出现在《诗经》(公元前11世纪到公元前6世纪)。早期旱魃带有神和怪二重的身份，它的形象特征是一位身穿绿色衣服的女子。从汉代后期开始，旱魃的形象开始转化为鬼。在山东地区，人们认为旱魃是死后一百天之内的人所变。在过去的山东，每逢遇到干旱，把新埋葬的尸体当做旱魃鬼打并烧的风俗十分普遍。在山东中部一些地区的乡村，烧旱魃的习俗甚至一直持续到20世纪60年代。

Hanba, also known as the Drought Demon, is a monster that is said to cause droughts according to ancient Chinese legends. The earliest written record of Hanba appeared in The Book of Songs (the oldest collection of Chinese poetry from the 11th century BC to the 6th century BC). In the early era, the Drought Demon had two identities: a god and a demon. Its symbolic representation was a woman wearing green clothing. Starting in the late Han Dynasty, the representation of Hanba had changed into a demon. In the Shandong region, people believed that Hanba were transformed within the first 100 days of a person's death. In ancient Shandong, every year when a drought occurred, it was a common custom to whip and burn the newly buried corpses, treating them as Hanba. In some villages in central Shandong, burning Hanba was a custom preserved to the 60s of the 20th century.

【一筹莫展 yì chóu mò zhǎn】

一筹莫展是一个成语。其中，"筹"的意思是办法，方法；"莫"的意思是不，没有；"展"的意思是施展，实施。一筹莫展的意思就是：一个办法也想不出来。

一筹莫展 is a Chinese idiom. 筹 means solutions or ways. 莫 means not or not have. 展 means to implement. Hence, the meaning of 一筹莫展 is to have not come up with a single solution.

【盘缠 pán chan】

"盘"在这里的意思是绕一圈。在中国古代，人们在出行的时候，会把钱和其他贵重的财物用布缠起来，绕一圈(也就是"盘")系在腰上。所以那个时候，人们出行时的路费或者旅费就叫做盘缠。现代汉语中，已经不用这个词表示路费或者旅费了。

盘 in here means to wrap around. In ancient China, when people were traveling, they would use a piece of fabric to wrap up money and other valuables, then wrap it around (hence the 盘) their waist. So back then, the travel expenses that people carried when they were traveling were called 盘缠. In modern Chinese, this word is no longer used to mean travel expenses.

该男子腰间就有一个盘缠 ➡

本插图选自《清末各样人物图册》，现藏于荷兰国立世界文化博物馆。

【衙役 yá yì】

在中国古代，政府机构的办事场所叫做衙门。在衙门里工作的员工就叫做衙役。衙役也分很多种类型，有些衙役专门负责文职工作，有些衙役需要负责抓捕工作。在现代中国，当然也已经不用衙门和衙役这两个词了。

In ancient China, the government agencies' workplace was called 衙门. The staff who worked in 衙门 was called 衙役. There were many types of 衙役. Some of them were responsible for paperwork, and some were responsible for arrest and capture work. In modern China, the terms 衙门 and 衙役 are no longer used.

【县令 xiàn lìng】

县令是中国封建社会时期的一个官职的名称。相当于现在的县长，市长。

县令 (county magistrate) was a position title in China's feudal society, equivalent to the present-day county or city mayor.

↑ 图为清朝官员服饰

本插图选自《清代文武官员品级图册》，清末 周培春 绘，
现藏于大都会艺术博物馆。

【报官 bào guān】

在中国封建社会，把政府叫做官府。报官的意思就是报告给官府。相当于现在的"报警"或者"向政府举报"。

In China's feudal society, the government was referred to as 官府. 报官 meant reporting to the government, equivalent to the modern concepts of "reporting to the authorities" or "informing the government."

【束手无策 shù shǒu wú cè】

"束"的意思是捆住，绑住；"策"的意思是对策，办法。那么，束手无策这个成语的意思就是：手好像被捆住了一样，一点办法都没有。

束 means to bind, be held up, or tied up. 策 means strategy or solution. As a result, 束手无策 is a Chinese idiom that means helpless or having no viable solution to a problem as if their hands were tied up.

【武林高手 wǔ lín gāo shǒu】

武林高手虽然是一个四个字的词汇，但它并不是一个成语。它是在近代才开始出现的词汇，表示的是功夫很厉害的人。比如李小龙，我们就可以叫他为武林高手。

Although 武林高手 is a four-character word, it is not an idiom. It is a term that appeared in recent times, meaning someone highly skilled in martial arts. For example, Bruce Lee could be called a 武林高手.

本插图选自《清末各样人物图册》，现藏于荷兰国立世界文化博物馆。

43

【鼓 gǔ】

鼓是一种打击乐器，一般为圆筒形，中间是空的。在中国的佛寺里，鼓是必不可少的一件东西。具有报时，召集寺内僧人等作用。有些佛寺里的鼓是非常大的，中间的空心部分足可以容纳一个人。有的时候还会专门建一个楼来放鼓，这样的楼就叫做鼓楼。

← 图为中国某寺庙里的一个大鼓

鼓 (drum) is a percussion instrument, usually cylindrical with a hollow center. In Buddhist temples in China, 鼓 is an indispensable item. It is used to announce time and gather monks in the temple. In some Buddhist temples, the drums are very big, with the hollow center spacious enough to accommodate a person. Sometimes, a dedicated tower is built to house the drum, and such a building is called 鼓楼 (Drum Building).

【自告奋勇 zì gào fèn yǒng】

自告奋勇是一个成语，指的是主动要求去完成某项任务。"自"- 自己，"告"- 表明，"奋勇"-鼓起勇气。

自告奋勇 is an idiom meaning to voluntarily step forward and offer to undertake a task. 自 means oneself, 告 means to declare, and 奋勇 means to gather courage.

孤魂野鬼
The Lonely Wandering Soul

本插图选自《书城十二图》，清代 邹一桂 绘，现藏于台北故宫博物院。

45

在唐朝有一个叫做郝惟谅的男人。他出身于贫苦人家，没有读过书，他性格粗心大意，但胆子却很大，没什么事能让他觉得害怕。

有一年清明节，他和朋友们去郊外游玩。他们一起踢蹴鞠，摔跤。玩累了就坐在草地上享用带来的食物和美酒。郝惟谅本来酒量很好，但那天不知道怎么回事，他没喝几杯就醉了。因为郝惟谅平日里总说自己"天不怕地不怕，鬼神来了也不怕"，所以朋友们就想趁此机会戏弄他一下。他们把郝惟谅抬到附近的一个墓地，把他放在那里后就离开了。

郝惟谅在墓地里一直睡到了半夜才醒来。夜色昏暗，他根本不知道自己身处何方，更没发现周围都是坟丘。他站起来，看到远处若隐若现的灯光，便朝那个方向走去。他的酒还没有全醒，就这么深一脚浅一脚地走了大约一刻钟，终于走到了有人烟的地方。

他走进了一个小村庄，觉得口渴难忍，想去要口水喝，也顺便问一下这里离他家所在的地方还有多远。只是时间太晚了，很多人家都已经关灯睡觉，他不好去打扰。

In the Tang Dynasty, there was a man named Hao Weiliang. He was born into a poor family and never had the opportunity to study. He had a careless personality, but he was very brave. There was nothing that could scare him.

On the day of the Qingming Festival one year, he and his friends were on an excursion. They were playing Cuju (similar to modern-day soccer) and wrestling. After getting tired from playing, they sat on the grassland and enjoyed the food and delicious drinks they brought with them. Hao Weiliang normally had a good tolerance for alcohol, but not quite sure what happened that day, he got drunk after only a few drinks. Because Hao Weiliang would always say that he "was not afraid of Heaven, nor Earth, and not even in the face of ghosts and gods," his friends wanted to play a prank on him. They moved Hao Weiliang to a nearby cemetery. After leaving him there, they left.

Hao Weiliang slept at the cemetery until midnight. The night was dark. He had no idea where he was and did not even notice that he was surrounded by tombstones. When he stood up, he saw lights vaguely flashing in not too far away, so he headed in that direction. He wasn't fully sober yet, so he walked unsteadily for about 15 minutes and finally arrived at a residential place.

He walked into a small village, feeling extremely thirsty, and wanted to drink some water. Also might as well ask to see how far this place was from his home. Except it was really late at night, so, many houses had already turned off the light and were sleeping, he felt embarrassed to bother them.

他又走了一会儿，眼看要走出村子了，他发现路边有一座还亮着灯的房子。房子十分低矮，虽然点着灯却仍然很昏暗。他刚敲响了门，木门就吱呀一声开了，仿佛里面的人就在门口等着一样。

郝惟谅没有进屋，而是在门口问道："打扰了，请问能给口水喝吗？"

里面传来一个女人的声音："进来吧！"这声音说不上来哪里有些奇怪。

郝惟谅走了进去。房子的构造十分简单，一进门就是客厅，左手边是一个厨房，右手边有一间卧室。屋里的家具都特别陈旧，一个女人正坐在客厅里的凳子上，她容貌憔悴，衣着破旧，神情透着一丝凄惨，正对着幽暗的烛火做着针线活。女子让郝惟谅先坐在椅子上休息，她走进厨房去倒水。

郝惟谅虽然不想偷看，但目光还是忍不住向卧室里瞟去。他隐约看到里面摆着一个长方形的东西，那东西怎么看怎么像是一个棺材。他用力地眨了眨眼，正想仔细看个究竟。那女人突然出现在他面前，她目光无神，整张脸甚至连嘴唇都是紫黑色的。她递

He continued walking for a while, and when he was about to exit the village, he noticed that on the side of the road, there was a house that still had its light on. The house was extremely short. Although the light was on, it was still dim. He barely knocked on the door, the wooden door creaked open as if the person inside was waiting for him.

Hao Weiliang didn't enter the house. Instead, he stood by the door and asked, "Excuse me, could you please get me some water to drink?"

A woman's voice came from inside, "Come in!" The voice sounded strange, but it was hard to pinpoint how.

Hao Weiliang walked inside. The structure of the house was very simple. Upon entering was a living room. To the left, there was a kitchen. To the right, there was a bedroom. The furniture in the house was particularly old. A woman was sitting on a chair in the living room. She appeared pale, wearing ragged clothes, and her eyes had a hint of sadness. She was facing the candlelight doing needlework. The woman had Hao Weiliang sit on the chair and rest while she went into the kitchen to pour water.

Although Hao Weiliang didn't want to peek, he couldn't help but look into the bedroom. He vaguely saw a rectangular thing in the room. That thing oddly looked like a coffin. He blinked his eyes hard, about to carefully examine it. That woman suddenly appeared in front of him. Her eyes appeared lifeless. Her entire face, even her lips, was dark purplish. She

给郝惟谅一碗水。郝惟谅接过碗，踌躇着不敢喝。

女人阴森森地开口："你不是要喝水吗？"

郝惟谅终于发现她的声音哪里奇怪了。这声音没有任何情感，冷冰冰得让人不禁打了个寒颤。更奇怪的是，屋里明明有两个人，但在烛火的映照下，却只见一个影子。

民间传言，鬼是没有影子的，郝惟谅已经意识到这女人是一个女鬼，但他还是直视着她的眼睛，直白地说："你……没有影子。"

女人也直勾勾地盯着郝惟谅，过了半晌，居然开始哭诉起来："我第一次见到您这么有胆量的人。请您帮帮我吧！我姓张，我的娘家在离这里很远的地方。我十八岁的时候嫁给了丈夫李自欢，然后就搬到这里来。结婚五年后，我丈夫被派去驻守边境，这一去就杳无音信，不知是死是活。后来我生病去世，在此地没有亲戚，邻居凑钱买了棺木给我，但却没有钱帮我下葬。已经过了12年了，我的棺材就这么停在卧室里。您知道，凡是死了的人，如果遗体没有埋进土里，阴魂就不被阴司收录。我就是一个孤魂野

handed a bowl of water to Hao Wei-liang. Hao Weiliang took the bowl, hesitating, and didn't dare to drink it.

The woman said with an eerie tone, "Don't you want to drink water?"

Hao Weiliang finally figured out why her voice was strange. This voice had no emotion. And it was so cold that it sent a chill throughout his body. Even oddly, there were two people in the house, yet under the candlelight, there was only one shadow.

According to folklore, ghosts did not have shadows. Hao Weiliang had already realized that this woman was a ghost, but he still looked straight into her eyes and said bluntly, "You... don't have a shadow."

The woman also stared straight at Hao Weiliang, and after a long time, she suddenly started crying and saying, "It is my first time seeing someone as brave as you. Please help me! My surname is Zhang. My hometown is in a place very far from here. When I was 18, I got married to my husband Li Zihuan, and then moved here. After five years of marriage, my husband was sent to serve at the border and there hasn't been any news from him since then. Not sure whether he is alive or dead. Later I got sick and passed away. I don't have any relatives here. The neighbors pooled in and bought a coffin for me, but they didn't have money to bury me. Twelve years have already passed since then, my coffin is still resting in the bedroom. As you know, after someone dies, if the body doesn't get buried

鬼，游荡在人间。今天是清明节，也没人祭奠我。请您可怜可怜我吧！让我的遗骨能够入土为安，结束这悲惨的一世，早日转世投胎。"

郝惟谅非常同情她，可是自己的财力有限，只好如实地说："我虽然有心帮你，但我家里贫寒，也没有钱帮你办葬礼。"

女鬼又说："我虽然是鬼，但一直都在帮本村的一个姓胡的富人家做针线活赚钱。这12年来，我一共攒了13万块钱，办个葬礼足够了。"

郝惟谅答应了她，然后就先回家了。第二天，他去胡家打听，果然这些年来胡家有请一个女人做针线活，但他们也不知道这个女人居然是一个鬼。她总是傍晚去取走针线活，第二天晚上再把绣好的衣物送回去。

underground, the soul won't get collected by the Underworld governing institution. So now I am a lonely wandering soul, wandering in the Human Realm. Today is the Qingming Festival, and no one has held a memorial ceremony for me. Please pity me! Bury my body in the ground so I can rest in peace, ending the misery of this lifetime, and reincarnate as soon as possible."

Hao Weiliang felt deep sympathy for her, but due to his limited financial resources, he had to tell her honestly, "Although I genuinely want to help you, my family is poor, and I don't have the money to organize a funeral for you."

The female ghost continued saying, "Although I am a ghost, I have been sewing for a wealthy family surnamed Hu and made money. These twelve years, I have gathered a total of 130,000 yuan, which should be enough to organize a burial."

Hao Weiliang agreed to her request and then returned home. The next day, he inquired at the Hu family's house. Indeed, over the years, the Hu family had employed a woman for sewing work, but they didn't know that the woman was actually a ghost either. She was always coming to pick up her work at midnight, and then the following night she would bring back the sewn garments.

郝惟谅和朋友们一起回到停放棺材的卧室，发现棺材外面有一堆零钱，钱数和女鬼所说的数目是一致的。他们既觉得很诧异，又觉得很可怜。于是又凑了一些钱，一共花了20万，隆重地举行了葬礼。举行葬礼后的那天晚上，女鬼出现在郝惟谅的梦里，向他行了个大礼后，她的身影像早上的薄雾一样，慢慢地消散了。

本故事改编自唐代小说集《酉阳杂俎》，作者段成式（公元803年-863年）。

Hao Weiliang and his friends returned together to the bedroom where the coffin was placed. They noticed a pile of coins outside the coffin. The amount of money matched what the female ghost had mentioned. They felt both surprised and sympathetic. So, they gathered some more money, totaling 200,000 yuan, and solemnly held the funeral. The night after the funeral, the female ghost appeared in Hao Weiliang's dream, she knelt and bowed to him. Then her silhouette slowly dissipated like the morning fog.

This story was an adaption of a story from the Tang Dynasty novel collection *Miscellaneous Morsels from Youyang* by the author Duan Chengshi (803 AD - 863 AD)

【清明节 qīng míng jié】

清明节是中国四大传统节日之一。一般在每年公历四月的4号，5号和6号的其中一天。扫墓祭拜祖先是清明节的重要内容之一。人们在这一天会回到祖先坟墓所在地，打扫祖先的坟墓，清除坟头上的杂草，烧纸钱，并在坟墓上摆上食物，烟酒，还有死者生前爱吃的食物或者喜爱的东西。清明节是一个严肃的，甚至有些伤感的节日。所以千万不要对中国人说"清明节快乐！"

The Qingming Festival is one of the four traditional Chinese festivals. It is normally on the 4th, 5th, or 6th of April in the Gregorian calendar. Cleaning the gravesites and making ritual offerings to ancestors are some of the most important parts of the Qingming Festival. On the day of, people will visit the gravesite of their ancestors. They will clean the tomb, remove any weeds growing on the tombstone, and burn joss paper. They will put food, tobacco, alcohol, and whatever favorite food or things that the deceased loved when they were alive on the tombstone as ritual offerings. The Qingming Festival is a serious and even a sad holiday, so make sure to not say "Happy Qingming Festival" to Chinese people.

⬆ 清明节，人们在坟墓上摆上食物祭奠祖先

除了扫墓，清明节还有踏青的习俗。"踏"的意思是踩踏，"青"指的是青草。清明节在春天，正是草地变成绿色的季节。一般传统的墓地都在郊外或者山上，所以在扫墓之后，人们会顺便去郊游，不仅祭拜了祖先，也要和还在世的家人们一起欢度时光。

Besides tomb sweeping, another Qingming Festival custom is 踏青 (outing). 踏 means to tread, and 青 refers to green grass. The Qingming Festival happens in spring — the very season when the grassland is turning green. Normally traditional cemeteries are on the outskirts or in the mountains, so after sweeping the tombstones, people will go on an outing. In doing so, they not only pay respect to their ancestors but also spend joyful time with the family members who are still alive.

【蹴鞠 cù jū】

"蹴"的意思是用脚踢，"鞠"是一种用皮革做的球。"蹴鞠"是一种体育活动，类似现在的足球。蹴鞠一词最早的文字记载出现在《史记·扁鹊仓公列传》(约公元前104年)。

蹴 means to kick using one's foot. 鞠 is a ball made using leather. 蹴鞠 is a sports activity, similar to modern-day soccer. The earliest record of the word 蹴鞠 appeared in Shiji, also known as The Records of the Grand Historian, circa 104 B.C.

本插图选自《仕女图卷》
明代 杜堇 绘
现藏于上海博物馆

⬆ 明代，正在踢蹴鞠的女子们

【酒量 jiǔ liàng】

"酒量"的"量"指的是数量，量度。酒量的意思就是一个人能喝酒的最大限度。比如，如果有人说"我的酒量就是一瓶啤酒"，他的意思就是他最多只能喝一瓶啤酒，再多喝的话就会醉。在中国很多地方，男人们以自己能喝很多酒却不会醉为傲，所以夸赞他们的时候就可以说："你酒量不错"，"你挺有酒量呀！"这样的话。一般中国北方人更擅长和喜欢饮酒，尤其是东北地区和山东省，人们的酒量普遍较大。

The character 量 in 酒量 refers to quantity or volume. 酒量 means one's capacity for alcohol. If someone says, "My 酒量 is a bottle of beer", it means that he can have a max of one bottle of beer. If he had more than one bottle, then he'd get drunk. In many places in China, men take pride in being able to drink a lot of alcohol without getting drunk. Therefore, when you give them compliments, you can say phrases like, "You can drink a lot" and "You have quite an alcohol tolerance!" Generally, people in northern China can drink a lot and enjoy drinking alcohol, especially in the northeast and Shandong Province, where people generally have a high alcohol tolerance.

【深一脚浅一脚 shēn yì jiǎo qiǎn yì jiǎo】

一脚踩在深的地方，另一脚踩在浅的地方。形容地面凹凸不平，或者天色昏暗看不清路。

One foot treads on a deep ground, while the other foot treads on a shallow ground. It describes the unevenness of the ground, or how the darkness makes it hard to see the road.

【人烟 rén yān】

人烟本来指的是人们在做饭的时候烧火而产生的烟，后面就广泛地指人所在的地方，人家，住所。

人烟 originally referred to the smoke produced by burning fires when people were cooking. Later, it has come to broadly refer to places where people reside, such as the town or their home.

【针线活 zhēn xiàn huó】

需要用针和线做的活，比如刺绣。

Work that requires a needle and threads, such as embroidery.

【娘家 niáng jia】

在古代汉语中，"娘"就是妈的意思。古代人对自己的母亲不叫"妈妈"，而是叫"娘"。娘家的意思就是女人自己的父母家。与此对应的是"婆家"，指的是丈夫的父母家。在现代汉语中，人们虽然不常用"娘"这个词来呼唤自己的母亲，但是还是会用到"娘家"这个词。比如可以说："我老婆回娘家了。"

In ancient Chinese, 娘 meant mother. Ancient Chinese people did not call their mother 妈妈, instead, they called them 娘. 娘家 means the woman's parents' home. In contrast, the term 婆家 refers to the woman's husband's parent's home. In modern Chinese, although people don't frequently use the word 娘 to call their mother anymore, the word 娘家 is still used. For example: My wife returned to her 娘家.

【杳无音信 yǎo wú yīn xìn】

杳无音信是一个成语。意思是：没有任何消息，了解不到对方的情况。

It is an idiom that means there is no news at all, not knowing the other person's situation.

【下葬 xià zàng】

"葬"指的是掩埋死人，泛指处理死者的遗体。在中国旧社会，人们一般会进行土葬，就是把死人放到棺材里，然后埋在土里。因为是向下埋到地下去，所以土葬也叫下葬。

葬 means to bury the dead, and in a broader sense, it means to handle the body of the deceased. In ancient Chinese society, people would normally carry out a burial, as in, putting the deceased in a coffin, and then burying them in the ground. Because the burial is performed by lowering the coffin, so 土葬 (bury in the ground) is also called 下葬 (bury by lowering).

新中国成立后，人口迅速增长，城市化进程加快，使用传统的土葬不仅会占用大量的土地空间，处理不好的尸体也会污染地下水资源，并且存在疾病传播的风险。从1997年开始，中国政府开始大力推广火葬，即把尸体烧成骨灰，放到骨灰盒里，之后再撒于水中或者埋到土里。目前，中国城镇居民的遗体基本已经全部采取火葬的方式进行处理。而在农村，仍有居民坚持采用土葬的方式处理祖先的遗体。

After the founding of New China (Translator's Note: New China refers to the People's Republic of China), the population grew rapidly, and the urbanization process accelerated. The use of traditional burials not only took up a lot of land space, but poorly disposed corpses could also pollute groundwater resources and carry the risk of disease transmission. Since 1997, the Chinese government has been vigorously promoting cremation, in which the body is burned as ashes and placed in an urn before being scattered in water or buried in the ground. At present, the remains of all residents of cities and towns in China have been mostly handled through cremation. In the countryside, however, there are still residents who insist on performing 土葬 to treat the remains of their ancestors.

【阴魂 yīn hún】【阴司 yīn sī】

根据中国道教神话传说，世界空间分为三个部分，也叫三界，分别是天庭，人间，和地府。

According to Chinese Taoist mythology, the world is divided into three parts, known as 三界 (three realms): Heaven, Human Realm, and the Underworld.

天庭，也写作天廷，即天上的宫廷，因此也被叫做天宫。是道教神话中最高的统治中心。只有神仙才能住在那里。

天庭 (Heaven), also written as 天廷, is the celestial palace in the sky. Therefore it is also known as 天宫 (Heavenly Palace). It is the highest ruling center in Taoist mythology. Only the gods can live there.

人间就是人生活的空间，也被叫做阳间。

人间 (The Human Realm) is the space where humans live, also known as 阳间.

地府，也被称为阴曹地府，或者阴间。人死了之后，灵魂就会去阴间。在阴间的政府机构叫做阴司。人在活着的时候，他的灵魂在自己的身体里，如果他死了，那么他的灵魂就会脱离肉体，去往阴间。所以人死后的灵魂就叫做阴魂。

地府 (Underworld), also known as 阴曹地府 or 阴间 (the Yin Realm). When a person dies, their soul goes to 阴间. The governing institution in the Underworld is called 阴司. When a person is alive, their soul resides in their own body. When they die, their soul separates from the body and goes to 阴间. Therefore, the soul of a person (which is 灵魂) after death is called 阴魂.

敦煌壁画中描绘的场景： ➡
经过地府的审判后，
有的人乘云去了天庭，
有的人去了地狱接受惩罚。

本插图选自《佛说十王经》
伯希和敦煌手稿
现藏于法国国家图书馆

【转世投胎 zhuǎn shì tóu tāi】

我们在上面解释"阴魂"这个词的时候讲过，人死后，人的灵魂会去阴间。如果这个人活着的时候做过坏事，那么到了阴间后他就要接受惩罚，罪越多越严重，惩罚就越严酷，接受惩罚的时间也越长。在接受过惩罚后，这个人的灵魂会再次投胎，也就是再次变成胎儿，出生到人间，开始他的下一世，即下一个人生。如果这个人活着的时候做过好事，那么他的下一个人生会更加幸福。

As we mentioned earlier when we explained the word 阴魂, after a person dies, their soul will go to the Underworld. If this person did something bad while alive, then they will face punishment in the Underworld. The more sins and the severer the sins, the harsher the punishment and the longer the duration of the punishment. After receiving the punishment, their soul will be reincarnated, that is, becoming a fetus and born again into the Human Realm to start their next life. In Chinese, next life is 下一世 or 下一个人生. If this person did good deeds while alive, then their next life will be happier.

敦煌壁画中描绘的场景: ➡
等待转世的人

本插图选自《佛说十王经》
伯希和敦煌手稿
现藏于法国国家图书馆

【孤魂野鬼 gū hún yě guǐ】

有的时候，有些特殊情况会导致某个人的灵魂无法去阴间。在这篇故事里，女子的尸体一直没有入土下葬，所以阴司无法判断这个女子的身份，也不知道她在活着的时候做过什么事，是应该惩罚她还是奖赏她。这就好像，去了新公司，但是没有带简历，也无法在系统中查到她之前的经历，所以就没有被"新公司"接收。女子的灵魂就只好孤独地在人间流浪，成为了一个"孤魂野鬼"。

在现代汉语中，孤魂野鬼也可以比喻那些没有依靠，处境艰难的人。比如："他在这里没有房子，没有亲人，也没有朋友。每天晚上，他就像一个孤魂野鬼一样，在城市里流浪。"

Sometimes, some special circumstances can prevent a person's soul from going to the Underworld. In this story, the woman's corpse was never buried in the ground, thus making it impossible for the governing institution in the Underworld to determine the woman's identity or know what she did when she was alive, and whether she should be punished or rewarded. It is like going to a new company, but not bringing a resume, and the system can't check her previous experience. As a result, she can't be accepted by the "new company". So the woman's soul has no choice but to wander alone in the Human Realm, becoming a "lonely wandering soul."

In modern Chinese, 孤魂野鬼 can also metaphorically refer to those without support, facing difficult circumstances. For example: He has no house, no relatives, and no friends here. Every night, he wanders through the city like a lonely wandering soul.

← 敦煌壁画中描绘的场景：
死后前往阴间的阴魂

本插图选自《佛说十王经》，
伯希和敦煌手稿，
现藏于法国国家图书馆。

【入土为安 rù tǔ wéi ān】

入土就是指土葬，人死后被埋入土中的意思。在上面"孤魂野鬼"这个词条中我们解释过，在过去，人的遗体被埋葬在土里是多么重要的一件事情。只有遗体被埋葬，死者的灵魂才能去阴间，留在人世间的亲人们也才能安心。

入土 is 土葬, where the deceased gets buried in the ground. As we explained in the term 孤魂野鬼, in the past, it was crucial for a person's remains to be buried. Only when the remains were buried, would the soul of the deceased be able to go to the Underworld, and their living relatives would feel peace.

【行了个大礼 xíng le ge dà lǐ】

行礼指的是用肢体语言表示敬意或者歉意。在不同的场合，不同的身份地位之间，行礼的方式也是不同的。在中国历史上的不同的朝代，行礼的姿势也不尽相同。

行礼 refers to expressing respect or apology through body language. In different situations, among people with different social statuses, the forms of 行礼 are also different. In the different dynasties in Chinese history, the forms of 行礼 also varied.

在古代，**行大礼**通常指的是跪拜。跪拜是一个非常隆重的礼仪。只有在拜神仙，皇帝和父母的时候才会跪拜。而且面对父母也不是经常要跪拜，非常特殊的场合才会行大礼。在本故事中，女鬼认为郝惟谅帮助自己转世投胎，相当于救命的恩情，所以才会行大礼。

正在向皇帝跪拜的官员 ➡

本插图选自《帝鉴图说》，约绘制于十八世纪，现藏于法国国家图书馆。

In ancient times, 行大礼 usually referred to kneeling and bowing to pay respect. Kneeling and bowing was a grand solemn ritual. Only when worshipping deities, the emperor, or parents do people kneel and bow. Even with parents, kneeling and bowing weren't common either. 行大礼 was only done on very special occasions. In this story, the female ghost believed that Hao Weiliang helped her reincarnate, which was equivalent to saving her life, so she performed such a grand gesture.

59

在现代中国，人们在拜佛的时候会跪拜，父母过世的时候会跪拜，中式传统婚礼的时候会跪拜父母，此外几乎就没有跪拜的场合了。还要注意的是，除了上述场合，中国人普遍认为跪是非常屈辱的姿势，所以有个成语叫做"膝下有黄金"，意思就是人要有志气，不能轻易对人屈膝下跪。这和韩国文化是很不同的，所以中国年轻人看到韩国人在过新年的时候除了对自己的父母，对其他的长辈或者观众也行跪拜礼会感到很诧异。

In modern China, people kneel and bow when worshipping Buddha, when their parents passed away, or kneel and bow to their parents during a traditional Chinese wedding. Aside from the mentioned occasions, the act of kneeling and bowing was quite uncommon. In addition, other than the mentioned situations, kneeling is generally considered extremely humiliating to Chinese people. There is an idiom 膝下有黄金 (beneath the knees lies gold), meaning a person should maintain one's dignity and not easily kneel to others. It is very different from Korean culture. This is why young Chinese people are surprised when they see Koreans kneel and bow not just to their parents during the New Year, but also to elders or an audience.

【酉阳杂俎 yǒu yáng zá zǔ】

《酉阳杂俎》是唐代作家段成式(公元803年-公元863年)创作的小说集。其中记录了很多民间流传的奇闻怪事。它其实不仅仅是一部小说集，它的内容涉及文学，历史学，民俗学，生物学，医药学，宗教学等领域，具有百科全书的性质，保存了唐代大量珍贵的历史资料。

《酉阳杂俎》 is a collection of stories written by the Tang Dynasty author Duan Chengshi (803 AD - 863 AD). It recorded many strange and supernatural phenomena passed down in society. It is not simply a collection of stories. Its content spans literature, history, folklore, biology, medicine, religion, and more, resembling an encyclopedia. The work preserves a wealth of valuable historical information from the Tang Dynasty.

冤鬼

The Vengeful Spirit

本插图选自《长江万里图》，南宋 夏珪 绘，现藏于台北故宫博物院。

夕阳已沉，一轮弯月低悬在江面上，奔流的江水在夜晚似乎流动渐缓。随着人流的散去，白天喧闹的瓜洲码头此刻陷入一片静谧之中。岸边只留下几艘在此过夜的小船，其中一艘便是段生租用的客船。

吃过晚饭后，划船的船夫早早就睡下了，段生却毫无睡意。他打开小窗向外看去，只见深沉的夜色和原野相连，远处江面那星星点点的灯光也不知道是星光还是渔火。风吹过岸边，吹得树叶沙沙作响，寒冷的空气涌进段生的房间里，让他不禁打了个寒战。他关上小窗，重新躺下，瞬间，孤独感像这寂静的夜晚从四面八方笼罩着他。他只好再次起身，拿出他随身携带的琴，在房内弹奏起来。

一曲还未弹完，他突然听到一声叹息。他以为自己把船夫吵醒了，然而探头一看，船夫仍在甲板上睡得正香。他又接着弹琴，没过一会儿，他清楚地听到了一声："唉！"他立刻停止弹琴，那叹息声也就没有了。他冲着外面问道："谁？"但却没有任何回应。

The sun was already set, and a crescent moon hung low over the river. The rushing river seemed to slow down at night. As the crowds dispersed, the bustling Guazhou wharf, once noisy during the day, now fell into silence. By the shore, only a few small boats moored for the night, one of which was the passenger boat rented by Duan Sheng.

After eating dinner, the boatman who rowed the boat had already fallen asleep, but Duan Sheng did not feel sleepy at all. He opened a small window and looked outside, only to see the deep night connecting with the wilderness. He wasn't sure whether the scattered lights on the river surface in the distance were starlight or lights on the boats. The wind blew by the shore, rustling the leaves, and the cold air rushed into Duan Sheng's room, causing him to shiver. He closed the window and lay back down. Instantly, a sense of loneliness enveloped him from all sides in this silent night. He had no choice but to get up again and take out the lute he carried with him, starting to play inside the room.

Before he could finish playing a piece, he suddenly heard a sigh. He thought he had awakened the boatman, but when he looked out, the boatman was still sound asleep on the deck. He then continued playing the lute. But shortly after, he clearly heard a sigh, "Oh!" He immediately stopped playing, and the sigh disappeared. He called out, "Who's there?" but there was no response.

这下他也没有弹琴的心思了，于是又躺下睡觉。不知辗转反侧了多久，他迷迷糊糊地看见一个二十多岁的陌生女子，她面色憔悴，衣衫褴褛，正蹲在他旁边，抚摸着他的琴，嘤嘤地低声哭泣。

"你是谁？"段生问。

"你的琴声真好听，像我父母弹得一样。"女子并未回答他的问题，而是自顾自地说着话。

段生又问道："你父母是谁？"

"我父母早就死了，说出来你也不知道。"

段生见她神态可怜，便柔声说道："你为何哭泣呢？"

"有歹人害死我，把我偷偷埋在这江岸边，然而我无依无靠，没人发现我失踪，也没人替我报官。我抱恨四十年，一直在人间游荡，此生仇未报，我不甘心啊！"

女子越说越面目狰狞，原本美丽的双眸也从眼眶里消失了，留下两个黑黢黢的洞口。段生感觉自己身体摇摆不受控制，好像要被那洞口吸进去了。他吓得大喊大叫起来。

Now he no longer had the mood to play the lute anymore, so he lay down to sleep again. After tossing and turning for who knew how long, he saw vaguely an unfamiliar woman in her twenties. She looked haggard, dressed in tattered clothes, squatting beside him, stroking his lute, and sobbing softly.

"Who are you?" Duan Sheng asked.

"Your lute playing was so pleasant, just like how my parents used to play," the woman didn't answer his question. Instead, she just said whatever she wanted.

Duan Sheng asked again, "Who are your parents?"

"My parents died a long time ago. You wouldn't know them even if I told you."

Seeing her pitiful expression, Duan Sheng spoke softly, "Why are you crying?"

"An evil person killed me and secretly buried me by the riverbank here. Since I had no one to rely on, no one noticed my disappearance or reported it to the authorities for me. I harbored the resentment for forty years, wandering in the mortal world. I refuse to accept leaving this life without seeking vengeance!"

The more the woman spoke, the more her expression became grotesque. Her once beautiful eyes disappeared from their sockets, leaving two dark black holes behind. Duan Sheng felt his body swaying uncontrollably as if being sucked into those black holes. He was so frightened that he screamed.

"公子！公子，你怎么了？"船夫听到他的叫声，在外面担心地问。

段生睁开双眼，原来刚才那是一场梦。他听到外面船桨拍打水面的声音，问船夫："我们已经离开瓜州了吗？"

"是的，公子。已经行船两个钟头了，我看您睡得香，就没有唤您起来。"

这一路小船顺风顺水，在夜幕降临之前便抵达了洛阳。段生这次来洛阳是为了拜访一个叫做樊元的朋友。樊元自幼学习法术，因此他有着一般人没有的能力，那就是他可以看见鬼神。

段生刚到樊元家，樊元就拉住他问道："段兄，怎么有一个女鬼跟着你呢？你路上有遇见什么怪事吗？"

段生把他梦见女鬼的事情一五一十地讲给樊元听。樊元安慰段生说："段兄别急，让我帮你把她赶走。"

说完，樊元拿出香烛，写了一张符咒，开始作法。不一会儿，平静的屋内突然刮起风来，那风一直在烛火面前打转。

"Young master! Young master, what's wrong?" The boatman heard his cry and asked worriedly from outside.

Duan Sheng opened his eyes, realizing it was just a dream. He heard the sound of oars hitting the water, and asked the boatman, "Have we left Guazhou?"

"Yes, young master. We've been sailing for two hours. Seeing you were sleeping soundly, I didn't wake you up."

The boat sailed smoothly all the way, and before nightfall, they arrived in Luoyang. Duan Sheng's visit to Luoyang this time was to visit a friend named Fan Yuan. Fan Yuan had been studying Taoist magic since childhood, so he had an ability that ordinary people didn't have: he could see ghosts and spirits.

As soon as Duan Sheng arrived at Fan Yuan's house, Fan Yuan grabbed him and asked, "Brother Duan, why is a female ghost following you? Did you encounter anything strange on the way?"

Duan Sheng recounted his dream about the female ghost to Fan Yuan in detail. Fan Yuan comforted Duan Sheng, saying, "Brother Duan, don't worry, let me help you drive her away."

With that said, Fan Yuan took out incense and candles, wrote a talisman, and started to perform the ritual. Soon, the calm room suddenly filled with wind, swirling around the candle flames.

樊元连忙拿出纸和笔，把它们丢到风里，只见毛笔在纸上飞舞起来，片刻，那张纸快速落到他们面前的桌子上。他们拿起来一看，整张纸上写满了字，看上去像是一首长诗。樊元又拿出一张纸，把上面的诗句抄写下来。因为据他所言，鬼写的字不久就会消失。果然，他刚把诗句抄下来，纸上就只剩下一块一块的污渍，再也没有字迹了。

他们凑到烛火前，一起看那女鬼写下的诗，这才了解到她的冤情。女子叫郑琼罗，父母双亡后，她一人去瓜州投靠亲戚。没想到还没找到亲戚，就在旅店里被当地一个官员的儿子强奸了。郑琼罗不堪凌辱，上吊自杀了。之后，她的魂魄难以安息，两次托梦给当地县令，请他为自己伸冤。但县令置之不理。郑琼罗不甘心就此放过歹人，一直游荡在阳间，等待机会报仇。

樊元和段生虽然同情郑琼罗的遭遇，但是他们二人无权无势，也不能帮助她报仇。樊元又去准备了酒，肉和纸钱，然后在路边把纸钱烧了，并劝女鬼说："善有善报，恶有恶报，不是不报，时候

Fan Yuan quickly took out paper and a brush pen, throwing them into the wind. The brush pen danced across the paper, and in a moment, the paper swiftly landed on the table in front of them. They picked it up and found the paper covered in writing, seeming like a long poem. Fan Yuan then copied the verses onto another piece of paper. Because according to him, words written by ghosts would vanish soon. Indeed, as soon as he finished copying, the paper was left with only splotches of stain, with no trace of the writing.

They gathered around the candlelight, and read the poem written by the female ghost together. Only then did they learn about her grievance. The woman's name was Zheng Qiongluo. After both of her parents died, she went to Guazhou to seek refuge with relatives. Unexpectedly, before she could find her relatives, she was raped by the son of a local official in an inn. Unable to bear the humiliation, Zheng Qiongluo committed suicide by hanging herself. Since then, her soul couldn't rest in peace. She visited the local magistrate twice in his dreams, asking for justice, but the magistrate ignored her pleas. Unwilling to let the evil person go unpunished, Zheng Qiongluo had been wandering in the mortal realm, waiting for an opportunity for revenge.

Although Fan Yuan and Duan Sheng sympathized with Zheng Qiongluo's plight, they had no power or authority to help her seek revenge. Fan Yuan prepared wine, meat, and hell money, then burned the hell money by the roadside, advising the female ghost, " Good deeds are rewarded, and e-

未到。"希望女鬼放下报仇的执念，早日去阴司报道，等待投胎转世。

他说完这些话后，一股旋风卷起纸灰，一直向上盘旋，空旷的原野上又听到哭泣声。哭声夹着女人哀怨的诗句：

痛填心兮不能语，

寸断肠兮诉何处？

春生万物妾不生，

更恨香魂不相遇。

意思就是：我的痛苦填满了我的心，但我却不能说出来。我悲伤难过到极点，就好像我的肠子被切断了一样，但是我能到哪里去诉说我这悲伤呢？春天到来，大地万物都复苏了，而我却不能复活。更遗憾的是，今日一别，我的灵魂就再也不能与您相遇了。

vil deeds are punished. If retribution or compensation does not come, it is because the time has not yet arrived." He hoped the female ghost would let go of her obsession with vengeance, depart for the underworld soon, and wait for reincarnation.

After saying these words, a whirlwind swept up the ashes of the burned hell money, spiraling upwards, and cries were again heard in the vast wilderness. The cries were accompanied by the sorrowful and spiteful verses of the woman:

"Pain fills my heart, but I cannot speak.

My heart is broken, but where can I tell?

Spring brings life to all, but not me.

What I resent even more, is that our souls cannot meet."

The meaning is: My pain fills up my heart completely, but I cannot express it. My grief is so deep that I feel like my gut is being cut. But where can I go to tell my sadness? Spring arrives and revives everything except me. What I lament even more is that after the goodbye today, my soul will never be able to meet yours again.

从那以后，女鬼就从段生身边消失了。但是去了哪里也没人知道。也许她已经放下仇恨，去往阴间。也许她还在世间游荡，等待报仇雪恨的那一天。

From then on, the female ghost disappeared from Duan Sheng's side. But where she went, no one knew. Perhaps she had let go of her hatred and departed for the underworld. Perhaps she still wandered in the mortal realm, waiting for the day to take her revenge.

本故事改编自宋代小说集《太平广记》，编撰年代为公元977年至978年。

This story is adapted from the Song Dynasty collection of stories *Taiping Guangji (Extensive Records of the Taiping Era)*, compiled between 977 and 978 AD.

【冤鬼 yuān guǐ】

"冤"的意思是没有任何原因地受到指责或者处分。我们常用的"冤枉"就表示无辜的人被诬陷为有罪，比如：这台电脑是我自己买的，不是我偷的，你不要冤枉我！

冤 means to be accused or punished without any reason. The commonly used term 冤枉 means that an innocent person is falsely accused of being guilty. For example: "I bought this computer myself. I didn't steal it. Don't 冤枉 me!"

故事里的"冤鬼"指的是被别人害死后，心中有怨念，希望伤害自己的人能够受到惩罚的鬼魂。

The 冤鬼 in the story refers to the ghost who was unjustly killed and held a grudge in her heart. She wanted the person who hurt her to be punished.

她和故事5中的孤魂野鬼不一样。孤魂野鬼是没有办法去阴间。而冤鬼是自己主动不愿意去阴间，也不愿意转世投胎，她一直留在人间，想要看到坏人受到惩罚，或者自己亲手惩罚坏人后，才愿意离开。（关于"阴间"，"转世投胎"的含义请看故事5后面的关键词解释）

She is different from the wandering soul in Story 5 (孤魂野鬼, gū hún yě guǐ, The Wandering Soul). The wandering soul was unable to go to the underworld, while this vengeful spirit was unwilling to go to the underworld or reincarnate. She stayed in the mortal realm and wanted to see the evil person punished, or would only leave after she had punished the evil-doer herself. (For the meaning of 阴间 and 投胎转世, please see the keyword explanations at the end of Story 5.)

【辗转反侧 zhǎn zhuǎn fǎn cè】

躺下后，不停地翻身，睡不着觉。

After lying down, tossing and turning nonstop, unable to fall asleep.

【自顾自 zì gù zì】

自己管自己的事。故事中"她自顾自地说话"就表示不管别人说什么或者问什么，她都只说自己想说的话。

Mind one's own business. In the story, 她自顾自地说话 means regardless of what others say or ask, she only says what she wants to say.

【歹人 dǎi rén】

"歹"的意思是不好，坏。"歹人"的意思就是坏人。一般口语中还是用"坏人"和"恶人"比较多。"歹人"更常用于书面语。

歹 means bad or evil. 歹人 means bad guy. In general, 坏人 and 恶人 are more commonly used in spoken language while 歹人 is more commonly used in written language.

【报官 bào guān】

是古代的报警的说法。具体可以看故事4后面的关键词解释。

The ancient way of saying to report to the police or the authorities. For more details, please refer to the keyword explanations in Story 4.

【县令 xiàn lìng】

县令是中国封建社会时期的一个官职的名称。相当于现在的县长，市长。

县令 was an official title in Chinese feudal society. It is equivalent to the current county mayor or city mayor.

【公子 gōng zǐ】

"公子"是在中国古代对年轻男性的一种尊称。

公子 is a respectful address for young men in ancient China.

【法术 fǎ shù】

法术指的是道教中，道士们用来招风唤雨，降魔除妖等的手段和方式。

法术 refers to the methods and techniques used by Taoist priests for purposes such as summoning wind and rain or warding off evil spirits and demons.

【段兄 duàn xiōng】

在中国古代，男性们会对比自己年纪大的其他男性尊称为"兄"或者"兄台"，"兄长"，也会把"兄"放在姓的后面一起说。比如故事中，"段兄"就是樊元用来尊敬地称呼段生时所说的。

In ancient China, men would respectfully address other men who were older than them as 兄 (older brother) or 兄台 (older brother), 兄长 (older brother), and also put 兄 after their last name. For example, in the story, 段兄 is what Fan Yuan used to respectfully address Duan Sheng.

【一五一十 yī wǔ yī shí】

一五一十是一个成语。比喻在讲述某一件事情的时候，从头到尾，没有遗漏。

一五一十 is a Chinese idiom. It means to tell something from beginning to end, without leaving anything out.

【符咒 fú zhòu】

道士在纸上写咒语，用于作法，也就是施展他的法力，比如驱除鬼怪，召唤风雨等。

Taoist priests write incantations on paper, which are then used to exercise their spiritual power, such as exorcising ghosts and demons, summoning wind and rain, etc.

⬆ 符咒示意图　　　⬆ 挂在某寻常人家门口的符咒，照片拍摄于2023年，中国云南

【善有善报，恶有恶报，不是不报，时候未到 shàn yǒu shàn bào, è yǒu è bào, bú shì bú bào, shí hou wèi dào】

这是一句常用的汉语俗语。意思是：做好事的人最终都会有好的回报，做坏事的人最终都会受到报应。如果你发现做坏事的人还没有受到惩罚，那么只是还没到惩罚他们的时间，他们早晚会受到惩罚的。

This is a common saying in Chinese. It means people who do good deeds will be rewarded, and people who do bad deeds will eventually be punished. If you see that people who have done bad deeds haven't been punished yet, it is simply because the time for punishment has not come yet. They will be punished sooner or later.

【托梦 tuō mèng】

在道教和中国民间信仰中，鬼和人是无法直接沟通的，除非和一些有特殊的能力人，比如像会法术的道士等。那么鬼如果想要和人交流，是可以出现在这个人的梦里，然后和这个人对话的。这种现象就叫托梦。

In Taoism and Chinese folk beliefs, ghosts and humans cannot communicate directly, except for some people who have special abilities. For example, Taoist priests who know how to exercise their spiritual power. So, if a ghost wants to communicate with a person, it can appear in their dreams and speak to them. This phenomenon is called 托梦.

【烧纸钱 shāo zhǐ qián】

"纸钱"就是用纸做的钱。在中国民间，人们认为人死了之后会去另一个世界生活，在那个世界里也是需要用到钱的。亲人们会燃烧纸钱给他们，让他们在那里花。

纸钱 is money made of paper (joss paper). In Chinese folk culture, people believe that after a person dies, they will live in another world, where money is also needed. Their relatives usually burn hell money for them to spend it there.

传统的纸钱就是一些纸上印着古时候的铜币，甚至只有第一页印有铜币，剩下的都是空白的纸。但这种纸和我们平时用的本子或者打印纸是不一样的。纸钱用的纸一般比较薄，容易燃烧，而且也没有经过多次漂白，纸张泛着黄色。新中国成立后，纸钱也有了更新换代，有些纸钱会按照人民币的款式印刷，但是面值会大很多，人民币的最大面值是100元，但是纸钱可能会印成1000元，10,000元，甚至十万元，等等。

Traditional hell money is simply paper printed with drawings of copper coins used in ancient society, and sometimes only the first piece of the paper is printed with copper coins, while the rest is blank. However, this type of paper is different from what we normally use for notebooks or printing. The paper used to print hell money is generally thinner, easy to burn, and has not been bleached much, so it tends to be yellow. After the founding of the People's Republic of China, hell money has also been updated, with some hell money notes printed imitating the design of China's legal currency (renminbi), but with much higher values. The highest value of renminbi is 100 yuan. But hell money can be printed with values of 1000 yuan, 10,000 yuan, or even 100,000 yuan, etc.

按照传统习惯，在清明节，祖先的忌日，阴历7月15日的鬼节，小年（阴历12月23日）以及一些其它的节日（每个地区的习惯都不太一样），都是需要给祖先烧纸钱的。一般在城市里，人们会在马路上烧纸钱；如果住在农村，人们会去坟地，或者在院子里烧纸钱。但是近年来，很多地方政府禁止民众烧纸钱。因为一方面，大范围地燃烧纸钱会污染空气；另一方面，在农村烧纸钱还会有引发山火的风险。所以，久而久之，烧纸钱这一习俗在一些家庭和城市里就慢慢地消失了。

According to traditional customs, on the Qingming Festival, the anniversary of the ancestors' death, the Ghost Festival, held on the 15th day of July according to the lunar calendar, Little New Year (December 23 on the lunar calendar), and some other festivals (customs vary in each region), hell money must be burned for their ancestors. Normally in cities, people burn hell money in the streets; if they live in villages, people usually go to the cemetery or burn hell money in the yard. However, in recent years, many local gove。rnments have prohibited people from burning hell money because, on the one hand, large-scale burning of hell money can pollute the air, and on the other hand, burning hell money in the countryside can cause forest fires. Therefore, over time, the custom of burning hell money is slowly disappearing in some families and cities.

钟馗杀鬼

Zhong Kui Kills Ghosts

本插图选自《钟馗图》，清代 吕学 绘，现藏于大英博物院。

靖康二年，洛阳城附近的一个村庄里来了一对流浪的父子。父亲年纪大约二十八九，衣着虽然陈旧，但却挺干净。他背着一个简陋的包袱，牵着一个5，6岁大的小男孩儿。他们二人睡在市场附近的一座小桥下。市场里卖菜的一个姓孙的老头看见他们很多次了，有的时候觉得他们可怜，就把卖剩下的黄瓜或者西红柿分给他们一些。父子二人总是特别有礼貌地鞠躬表达感谢。

这么一来二去，市场里的人和这对父子也熟络了，得知男子姓赵名龙，妻子和其他的孩子都死于战乱中，只留下小儿子赵佳明，二人从开封逃难而来。赵龙在市场里找了个力气活儿，帮卖菜的商贩给大户人家送货，去送货的时候他就把儿子赵佳明留在卖菜老头的摊位旁。

有一天，赵龙送货回来，看见卖菜的孙老头正急得团团转，原来刚才来了很多人买菜，老头忙活完之后才发现站在摊子旁的佳明不见了。

In the Second Year of Jingkang, a pair of wandering father and a son arrived in a village near Luoyang. The father, about twenty-eight or twenty-nine years old, was dressed in old but clean clothes. He carried a rough sack on his back and was holding the hand of a boy about five or six years old. They slept under a small bridge near the market. An old man surnamed Sun, who sold vegetables in the market, had seen them many times. Sometimes feeling sorry for them, he would give them some leftover cucumbers or tomatoes. The father and son always bowed politely to express their gratitude.

Over time communicating like so, the people in the market became acquainted with this father and son. They learned that the man's name was Zhao Long. His wife and other children had died in the war, leaving only his youngest son Zhao Jiaming. The two of them had fled from Kaifeng City to take refuge. Zhao Long found a labor job in the market helping the vegetable vendors deliver goods to wealthy households. When he went to deliver goods, he would leave his son Zhao Jiaming by the old vegetable vendor's stall.

One day, when Zhao Long returned from delivering goods, he saw old man Sun in a state of panic. It turned out that many people had come to buy vegetables, and after the old man busily finished, he discovered that Jiaming, who had been standing by the stall, was missing.

赵龙急坏了，疯了一般四处寻找儿子，周围认识的好心人也帮他一起寻找。他们边喊着佳明的名字，边询问路过的人有没有看到一个五六岁的小男孩。终于在市场不远处的一座房子前发现了佳明。赵龙一把抱起儿子，嘴里禁不住责怪到："佳明！爹不是跟你说过不要乱跑的吗？！"

Zhao Long became frantic, searching everywhere for his son. The good people he knew in the market also helped him search. They shouted Jiaming's name and asked passersby if they had seen a five or six-year-old boy. Finally, not far from the market, they found Jiaming in front of a house. Zhao Long picked up his son, unable to restrain himself from scolding, "Jiaming! Didn't I tell you not to run around?"

佳明委屈地说："有个红衣服的姐姐让我跟她一起走的呀！"

Jiaming, feeling wronged, said, "A lady in a red dress asked me to go with her!"

"什么红衣服的姐姐？"

"What lady in a red dress?"

"就是一个漂亮姐姐，她刚刚还在这里的，怎么不见了呢？好像走进这栋房子里去了。"

"A pretty lady. She was just here. When did she disappear? It seems like she went into this house."

人们这才开始仔细打量眼前的房子，瞬间大惊失色，纷纷慌忙离去。卖菜的老头也赶紧拉着父子二人离开："快走吧！这是凶宅啊！"

Only then did people start to carefully examine the house in front of them. In an instant, they were shocked and turned pale, hastily leaving one after another. Even the old man selling vegetables hurriedly pulled the father and son away, saying, "Let's go quickly! This is a haunted house!"

赵龙不解："什么凶宅？"

Zhao Long puzzled, "What haunted house?"

老头怕吓到小孩子，压低声音在赵龙耳边说："这一家人都被仇家杀了，上上下下二十多口人哪，一个活口都没留！也不知道有什么仇，每个人都被砍了几十刀，血流成河呀！"

The old man, afraid of scaring the child, whispered in Zhao Long's ear, "The whole family in this house was killed by enemies. More than twenty people, not a single survivor! It's unclear what kind of grudge they had against the family. Each person was stabbed dozens of times, and blood flowed like a river!"

"那也没有亲戚接管这所房子吗？"

"Wasn't there any relative to take over this house?"

"怎么没有！这么一个大宅子谁看着不眼馋呢！一开始是他家的一个远方亲戚过来清扫，然后住了进去，不久后，家里莫名其妙地开始死人，一个接一个的，他们发现情况不对，就连夜搬走了。后来啊，一些胆大的人也尝试搬进去住，要么会没有理由地死掉，要么就被吓疯了，说是半夜闹鬼呢！"

"Naturally! Who wouldn't covet such a big mansion? At first, a distant relative of the family came to clean it up and moved in. But not long after, people in the family inexplicably started dying, one after another. When they realized something was wrong, they moved out overnight. Later, some brave souls tried to move in, either dying for no reason or becoming crazy from fear, saying it was haunted at night!"

"那这房子现在没人住吗？"

"So, is nobody living in this house now?"

"是啊！十里八乡的都知道这凶宅的厉害了！哪个不要命的还敢住啊？"老头说到这感觉有点不对劲儿，赶忙拉住赵龙，说道："我说佳明他爹啊！你不会打这个房子的主意吧？你不要命啦？"

"Of course! Everyone within the miles knows how dangerous this haunted house is! Who would dare to live there?" The old man felt something was off as he spoke and hurriedly stopped Zhao Long, saying, "Hold on, Jiaming's father, you're not thinking of taking over this house, are you? Are you trying to get yourself killed?"

赵龙不好意思地笑了一下，解释说："白住别人家的房子是不太好。但是，眼看天越来越冷了，我倒是能坚持，可是佳明还小，冬天睡在桥下面非冻坏不可。我们就先住进去，过了冬天再搬出来。"

Zhao Long smiled apologetically and explained, "It's not good to live in someone else's house for free. But, seeing how the weather is getting colder, I can endure it, but Jiaming is still young. He'll freeze sleeping under the bridge in winter. We'll move in first and leave after winter."

老头急得说话都结巴了，但是任他怎么劝，还是说服不了赵龙。当天傍晚赵龙就带着儿子住进了凶宅。房子里不仅家具齐全，连碗筷和被褥都有很多副。佳明住进大房子里很开心，从这个房间跑到那个房间，快乐地唱个不停。老头忧心忡忡地，也壮着胆子跟了进来，在每个房门上都贴了一幅画，看天色慢慢全黑了，他急匆匆地离开了。

看到孙老头走了，佳明问他父亲说："爹！孙爷爷为什么在每扇门上都贴上一个丑八怪呀？"

"这是钟馗。你回到床上躺好，爹就给你讲钟馗的故事。"

佳明迅速躺到床上，他太喜欢听父亲讲故事了。

"相传在唐朝啊，有一位皇帝叫唐玄宗。他有一次得了重病，请了很多太医都查不出他的病因来。有一天晚上，唐玄宗昏昏沉沉地睡着了，忽然听到一阵嘻嘻哈哈的笑声，他睁眼一看，看见一个小鬼，个子不高，长着一个牛鼻子，穿着一件红色衣服，一只脚穿着鞋，一只脚光着。小鬼一蹦一跳来到唐玄宗的书桌前，取下唐玄宗的玉笛玩耍，发出嘻嘻哈哈的笑声。唐玄宗很生气，

The old man was so frantic that he began to stutter, but no matter how hard he tried to persuade him, he couldn't convince Zhao Long. That evening, Zhao Long moved into the haunted house with his son. Not only was the house fully furnished, but there were also plenty of utensils and bedding. Jiaming was very happy to move into the big house, running from one room to another, singing happily nonstop. The old man, worried, bravely followed them in and hung a painting on each door. As it grew dark, he hurriedly left.

Seeing the old man leave, Jiaming asked his father, "Dad! Why did Grandpa Sun put a painting of an ugly person on every door?"

"That's Zhong Kui. Go back on the bed and lie down well. I'll tell you the story of Zhong Kui."

Jiaming quickly lay down on the bed. He loved listening to his father tell stories.

"It is said that during the Tang Dynasty, there was an emperor named Tang Xuanzong. He once fell seriously ill and despite consulting many doctors, none could diagnose his illness. One night, while Tang Xuanzong was dozing off, he suddenly heard mischievous laughter. He opened his eyes and saw a little ghost, short in stature with a bull's nose, dressed in red clothes, one foot shod and the other barefoot. The little ghost hopped to Tang Xuanzong's desk, took his jade flute, and played with it, laughing mischievously. Tang Xuanzong was angry and was about to call the impe-

正想要大声呼喊侍卫，一个身材高大的怪物突然冲进屋里。这大怪物头上戴着一顶破帽子，身上穿着一件蓝色的长袍。他长得又高又壮，腰上系着的腰带感觉都不够长，快要挣开了。那小鬼见到他吓得慌忙逃窜，只见他大步流星，一下子就捉到了小鬼，用食指一挑挖出来小鬼的眼睛，扔到嘴里吃了。然后，又把小鬼撕成两半，咔嚓咔嚓地像吃胡萝卜一样都吃掉了。吃完他还擦擦嘴，瞥见目瞪口呆的唐玄宗，这大鬼居然开口解释说，他叫钟馗，生前因长相丑陋不受待见，内心羞愧撞台阶而死，死后就成了鬼王，专门负责抓游荡在人间的恶鬼。还让唐玄宗放心，他会为皇帝除尽这世间的妖魔鬼怪。"

佳明听得又害怕又觉得有趣，见父亲讲完了故事，追问到："那个大鬼就是孙爷爷贴在门上的那个丑八怪吗？"

"正是，那就是钟馗像。当年唐玄宗醒来后，感觉神清气爽，病全都好了。他马上召见大画家吴道子，让他根据自己晚上见到的场景，画了一张图，名为钟馗捉鬼图。并将此图挂在门上，用以镇妖除邪。后来民间也开始流行挂钟馗当门神了。"

rial guards when a tall monster suddenly rushed into the room. This tall monster wore a tattered hat and a blue robe. He was tall and strong. His belt barely fit his waist and seemed to be about to come undone. The little ghost, seeing him, fled in panic, but he quickly caught the little ghost, plucked out its eyes with his index finger, ate them. Then he tore the little ghost in half and ate it like eating carrots. After he finished chewing, he wiped his mouth. Seeing Tang Xuanzong stunned, surprisingly, this big monster explained that his name was Zhong Kui. When he was alive, he was disdained for his ugly appearance. He was so ashamed that he committed suicide by hitting the stairs. After his death, he became the Ghost King, specializing in catching evil spirits roaming in the human world. He also reassured Tang Xuanzong that he would help the emperor rid the world of demons, ghosts, and monsters."

Jiaming listened, feeling both scared and intrigued. When his father finished the story, he asked, "Is that big monster the very ugly person in the drawing that Grandpa Sun put on the door?"

"Exactly, that's Zhong Kui's portrait. When Tang Xuanzong woke up, he felt refreshed, and his illness was completely gone. He immediately summoned the great painter Wu Daozi and asked him to paint a picture based on the scene he saw that night, naming it 'Zhong Kui Captures Ghosts.' He hung this portrait on the door to ward off evil. Later, it became popular among the people to hang Zhong Kui as a door god to protect the house."

"我懂了，要是有鬼来敲门，钟馗就会从画里跳出来抓它们对不对？所以孙爷爷在每扇门上都挂了钟馗。"

"Now I understand. If ghosts come knocking, Zhong Kui will jump out of the painting and catch them, right? That is why Grandpa Sun hung Zhong Kui's portrait on every door."

"这只是民间传说。佳明，爹跟你讲，这世界上就没有鬼，鬼是人们想象出来的东西。快睡吧。"

"That's just a folk legend. Jiaming, let me tell you. There are no ghosts in this world. Ghosts are things people imagine. Now, go to sleep."

熄灯不久后，赵龙就睡着了。赵佳明也想睡觉，但却睡不着，他还惦记着孙爷爷白天给他买的方糕，父亲只让他吃了一块，剩下的还放在客厅的桌子上。他悄悄爬起来，溜进客厅里，准备偷吃一块方糕。客厅的门没有关严，一阵风吹过，吹得门吱呀一声开了。外面月色明亮，赵佳明看到白天见过的那个红衣姐姐正站在院子里冲他招手。他白天觉得这个姐姐漂亮极了，但是在夜晚，他感觉姐姐的脸看起来有些可怕。他正犹豫着要不要出去，一个高大的怪物不知道从哪里冒了出来，他长得又高又壮，穿着长袍，系着腰带。他三步并作两步，抓住红衣女鬼，扔进嘴里吃掉了。

Shortly after the lights were extinguished, Zhao Long fell asleep. Jiaming also wanted to sleep, but he couldn't. He was still thinking about the rice cakes Grandpa Sun bought for him during the day. His father only let him eat one piece, and the rest were left on the table in the living room. He quietly got up and sneaked into the living room, planning to steal and eat a piece of the rice cake. The living room door wasn't closed properly, and a gust of wind blew it open with a creak. Outside, under the moonlight, Jiaming saw the lady in the red dress he had seen during the day waving at him in the yard. He thought she was very pretty during the day, but at night, her face seemed a bit scary. He hesitated whether to go out when a tall monster appeared out of nowhere. He was tall and strong, wearing a long robe and a belt. He quickly caught the female ghost in the red dress, threw her into his mouth, and ate her.

赵佳明看到这可怕的场景，连忙跑回卧室，哭着叫醒父亲。父亲安慰他说，一定是他听完鬼故事后做噩梦了，这世界上根本没有鬼。

Seeing this terrifying scene, Jiaming hurried back to the bedroom, crying and waking up his father. His father comforted him, saying he must have had a nightmare after listening to the ghost story, and there were no ghosts in this world.

父子二人再次睡着后，院子里又陷入一片寂静之中。微风吹动门上的画像，画像里的虬髯大汉似乎笑了一下。

本故事中关于唐玄宗与钟馗的情节改编自北宋时期的一部著作《梦溪笔谈》，作者沈括，生卒年代：1031年-1095年。

另，本故事中关于赵龙和赵佳明的情节为本书作者创作。

After the father and son fell asleep again, the yard fell into silence once more. A gentle breeze rustled the portrait on the door, and it seemed that the bearded man in the portrait smiled.

The plot of the story about Tang Xuanzong and Zhong Kui is adapted from a work called *Dream Pool Essays* written by Shen Kuo during the Northern Song Dynasty, who lived from 1031 to 1095.

The plot featuring Zhao Long and Zhao Jiaming in this story is created by the author of this book.

【靖康二年 jìng kāng èr nián】

在中国封建社会，不用公元来记录年份，而是使用一种叫做年号的方式来记录年份。年号就是年的名称，通常为两个字，也有少数情况会有三个字甚至四个字，这个名称一般由皇帝决定，比如本故事中，靖康就是北宋的一位皇帝宋钦宗使用的年号，那么纪年的方式就是靖康一年，靖康二年，以此类推。只可惜这位皇帝只在位了两年，新皇帝即位时为了和上一个皇帝进行区分，都会更改年号。就像宋钦宗退位后，新皇帝宋高宗就改年号为建炎。

In the Chinese feudal society, years were not recorded using the Gregorian calendar, but rather by a system called 年号 (nián hào, era name). 年号 is the name of the year, typically consisting of two characters, although there are rare cases of three or even four characters. This name is usually decided by the emperor. For example, in this story, 靖康 (jìng kāng) was the era name used by Emperor Song Qinzong of the Northern Song Dynasty. Therefore, the way to express a year is 靖康一年 (First Year of Jingkang), 靖康二年 (Second Year of Jingkang), and so on. Unfortunately, this emperor only reigned for two years. When a new emperor ascended the throne, they would change the era name to differentiate their reign from the previous emperor. Just like after Song Qinzong abdicated, the new emperor, Song Gaozong, changed the era name to 建炎 (jiàn yán).

有些皇帝在位时只会使用一个年号，有些皇帝则会使用很多个。这是因为，如果遇到一些大事，无论是好事还是灾祸，君王都有改年号的习惯。例如故事中的皇帝唐玄宗一共用了3个年号。第一个年号为先天，该年号一共用了两年，那么纪年方式就是：先天一年，先天二年。之后唐玄宗改了年号，新的年号为开元，开始重新纪年：开元一年，开元二年，开元三年，一直到开元二十九年。后面，他又改了个年号为天宝，这个年号用了十五年，直到下一个皇帝登基。

Some emperors only used one era name during their reign, while others used many. This is because kings had the habit of changing the era name in the event of significant events, whether they were auspicious or disastrous. For example, Emperor Tang Xuanzong of the Tang Dynasty, mentioned in the story, used a total of three era names. The first era name was 先天 (xiān tiān), which lasted for two years. Therefore, the way to express the years was 先天一年 (First Year of Xiantian), and 先天二年 (Second Year of Xiantian).

Later, Tang Xuanzong changed the era name to 开元 (kāi yuán), starting a new era: 开元一年 (First Year of Kaiyuan), 开元二年 (Second Year of Kaiyuan), 开元三年 (Third Year of Kaiyuan), and so on until 开元二十九年 (Twenty-ninth Year of Kaiyuan). Later, he changed the era name again to 天宝 (tiān bǎo), which lasted for fifteen years until the next emperor ascended the throne.

公元1911年，孙中山领导的国民党军队推翻了中国的最后一个封建朝代，建立了中华民国，废除了皇帝起名的帝制年号，并把公元1912年1月1日作为中华民国的元旦，所以公元1912年在那时候叫做民国一年，1913年叫做民国二年，以此类推。后来，国民党在内战中失利，退守台湾。共产党在公元1949年成立了今天的中华人民共和国，并开始和国际接轨，使用公元来记录年份。而台湾目前则依然使用民国来纪年。

In 1911 AD, the Nationalist Party led by Sun Yat-sen overthrew China's last feudal dynasty, establishing the Republic of China and abolishing the imperial era names. They adopted January 1, 1912, as the New Year's Day of the Republic of China. Therefore, in 1912 AD, it was called the first year of the Republic, in 1913 AD, it was called the second year of the Republic, and so on. Later, the Nationalist Party was defeated in the civil war and retreated to Taiwan. The Communist Party founded the People's Republic of China in 1949 AD and began to align with international standards, using the Gregorian calendar to record years. However, Taiwan still uses the Republic of China (民国) era system to record years.

【鞠躬 jū gōng】

鞠躬是一种身体动作，具体为向前弯下身子，以此表示尊敬，歉意或者屈服。在中国，这一礼节形式起源于商代（公元前1600年-公元前1046年）。根据春秋战国时期（公元前770年-公元前221年）的书籍记载，那时候的人们在参加庆典时就要行鞠躬礼。在唐朝以后，鞠躬礼已经普遍流传开来，它既适用于庄严的场合，又适用于普通的社交场合。

鞠 躬 is a bodily gesture, specifically bending forward to show respect, apology, or submission. In China, this form of etiquette originated from the Shang Dynasty (1600 BC - 1046 BC). According to records from the Spring and Autumn Period (770 BC - 221 BC), people would perform this bow during ceremonies. After the Tang Dynasty, the bowing gesture became widespread, suitable for solemn occasions as well as ordinary social interactions.

随着时代的变迁，现在的中国人在日常生活中已经不再行鞠躬礼，一些极特殊的场合才会有。但在汉文化圈的其他国家，比如韩国和日本，鞠躬礼在日常生活中仍然应用的十分广泛。

Over time, modern Chinese people no longer perform the bowing gesture in their daily lives, reserving it for extremely special occasions. However, in other countries within the Sinosphere, such as Korea and Japan, bowing remains a widely practiced etiquette in daily life.

← 古画中正在互相鞠躬的两人

本插图选自《太平春市》，清代 丁观鹏 绘，现藏于台北故宫博物院。

【急得团团转 jí de tuán tuán zhuàn】

在这个常用表达里，"团"的意思是"圈"。急得团团转：着急地转了一圈又一圈。就是非常着急的意思。

In this commonly used expression, 团 means circle. 急得团团转 describes someone being so anxious that they spin around in circles, indicating extreme impatience.

【爹 diē】

爹就是父亲。古时候在呼唤自己的父亲时，不用爸爸，而是用爹。现在也依然有人这么称呼，尤其是在农村地区。

爹 means father. In ancient times, instead of 爸爸, people used 爹 to call their fathers. Some people still use this term, especially in rural areas.

【大惊失色 dà jīng shī sè】

大惊失色是一个成语。其中，色的意思是脸色，神色；惊的意思是吃惊，惊讶。那么大惊失色就是：非常吃惊，连脸色都失常了。形容一个人极度惊恐。

大惊失色 is a Chinese idiom. 色 refers to facial color or expression, while 惊 means surprised or astonished. 大惊失色 means being extremely surprised, to the extent that one's facial color changes abnormally. It describes a person being extremely terrified.

【凶宅 xiōng zhái】

凶，凶杀；宅，房子。凶宅指的是发生过凶杀，意外死亡或者闹鬼等的房屋。

凶 means murder or ominous, and 宅 means house. 凶宅 refers to a house where murders, accidental deaths, or hauntings have occurr-ed.

【十里八乡 shí lǐ bā xiāng】

十里八乡，或者十里八村，是一个汉语俗语。"里"是中国计量距离的单位，目前也在使用，一里等于500米。十里八乡的字面含义是：附近十里距离内的八个村子。但是它的准确含义并不是说具体的距离和村庄的数量。而是表示：附近的一些村庄，附近的一些地方。

十里八乡, or 十里八村 (shí lǐ bā cūn), is a Chinese idiom. 里 is a unit of distance in China, currently still in use, with one 里 being equal to 500 meters. The literal meaning of 十里八乡 is eight villages within ten li. However, its precise meaning is not about the specific distance or the number of villages. It is used to express "nearby villages or places."

【钟馗 zhōng kuí】

中国民间传说中一个知名的人物。在道教里，钟馗是一个神，能够捉鬼。中国民间常把带有钟馗像的画挂在门上，能够辟邪除灾。这一习惯不仅在中国古代流行，在现代也很常见。有一些地区，还会在春节，端午，商店开业，婚礼等重要庆典上，悬挂钟馗画像。

钟馗 is a well-known figure in Chinese folklore. In Taoism, Zhong Kui is a god known for capturing ghosts. It is common in Chinese folklore to hang portraits of Zhong Kui on their doors to ward off evil spirits. This tradition was popular not only in ancient China but also in modern times. In some regions, paintings of Zhong Kui are hung during important celebrations such as the Spring Festival, Dragon Boat Festival, shop openings, weddings, and other important ceremonies.

⬆ 民间悬挂在家里的钟馗像，大约绘制于19世纪末，20世纪初。

85

【丑八怪 chǒu bā guài】

表示相貌丑陋的人。

Refers to someone with a very ugly appearance.

【唐玄宗 táng xuán zōng】

唐玄宗是中国历史上非常知名的一位皇帝。他出生于公元685年，死于公元762年。他一共当了45年的皇帝，是唐朝在位最久的皇帝。他治国有方，带领唐朝进入了发展的全盛时期。但他在位的后期，重用奸臣，沉迷女色，整日饮酒作乐，使得唐朝由盛转衰。

Emperor Tang Xuanzong is a very well-known emperor in Chinese history. He was born in 685 AD and died in 762 AD. He reigned as emperor for a total of 45 years, making him the longest-reigning emperor of the Tang Dynasty. He governed the country well, leading the Tang Dynasty into a period of prosperity. However, in the later years of his reign, he trusted disloyal officials and gave them important positions. In addition, he indulged in pleasures with women and spent his days drinking and reveling, leading to the decline of the Tang Dynasty from prosperity to downfall.

有关唐玄宗的生平事迹被翻拍成多部电视剧和电影，尤其他和杨贵妃的故事更是在中国家喻户晓。

The life story of Emperor Xuanzong has been adapted into numerous television dramas and films, especially the story between him and his concubine Yang Guifei, which is widely known in China.

← 古代画像中的杨贵妃
本插图选自《古代美人图》，清末 周培春 绘
现藏于圣彼得堡国立大学图书馆

【太医 tài yī】

在封建社会，专门为皇帝，皇帝的家人和高级官员看病的医生就叫做太医。

In feudal society, 太医 refers to physicians who specialize in treating the emperor, members of the imperial family, and high-ranking officials.

【大步流星 dà bù liú xīng】

大步流星是一个成语，形容脚步迈得很大，走得很快。

大步流星 is an idiom describing someone walking with large steps, moving swiftly.

【目瞪口呆 mù dèng kǒu dāi】

"目"是眼睛；"瞪"表示睁大眼睛直视；"口"是嘴巴；"呆"的意思是发呆，发愣。目瞪口呆的含义就是：因为吃惊或者害怕而呆在原地。

目 means eyes. 瞪 means to widen one's eyes to stare. 口 is mouth. 呆 means to be absent-minded or dazed. The phrase 目瞪口呆 means being dumbfounded or stunned in place due to surprise or fear.

【方糕 fāng gāo】

方糕是一个中国传统糕点，在宋代非常流行。它用糯米包裹着各种甜味的馅料，比如芝麻，豆沙等。因为形状是方形，所以叫做方糕。

A traditional Chinese pastry that was popular during the Song Dynasty. It consists of glutinous rice wrapped around various sweet fillings such as sesame, bean paste, etc. Because of its square shape, it is called 方糕 (square cake).

【吴道子 wú dào zǐ】

吴道子，唐朝人。中国历史上的著名画家，被称为画圣。

Wu Daozi was a famous painter in Chinese history in the Tang Dynasty, renowned as the Sage of Painting.

← 相传为吴道子画作的宋代临摹品

本插图选自《送子天王图》
原画为唐代 吴道子 绘
本画作为宋代临摹品
现藏于大阪市立美术馆

【三步并作两步 sān bù bìng zuò liǎng bù】

字面意思是：把本来应该走三步的距离用两步来走完。表示步子迈得很大，走得快。和前面的大步流星是近义词。

The literal meaning is completing a distance that should take three steps in just two steps. It implies walking very quickly. It is a synonym for the previous phrase 大步流星.

【虬髯 qiú rán】

卷曲且浓密的络腮胡。

curly and thick beard

狐狸精

The Fox Spirit

本页插图选自《聊斋全图》第九册，清光绪时期绘本，现藏于奥地利国家图书馆。

从前有一个男人，名叫董遐思，是山东青州人。山东的冬天很寒冷，在过去，人们需要在家里烧碳火取暖，尤其是夜幕降临后，更是要在床铺旁边点上碳火，不然被窝里一定是冷冰冰的。

某个冬日，夕阳刚刚西沉，董遐思就把炭火添旺，把床上的被子铺好，刚要去点灯，他的朋友就来找他一起去喝酒。于是，他锁上了门，跟着朋友离开了。

二人到了小酒馆，坐下没喝几杯，就看到旁边的桌子围了一群人，很是热闹。他们俩也过去凑热闹，原来是有一位医生坐在那里喝酒，他说他可以通过号脉去判断人的寿命有多长，众人很好奇，排着队让那医生挨个号脉。

董遐思和他的朋友也拜托医生给他们号脉。那医生给董遐思号脉之后脸上露出了讶异的神情，他说："找我号脉的人可以说是数不胜数，但我从来没见过董先生你这样奇特的脉象了！看上去本应该是长寿的脉，但是不知道为何却有短命的征兆。"周围的人都吃惊地询问其中的缘由。医生摇着

Once upon a time, there was a man named Dong Xiasi, from Qingzhou, a city in the Shandong Province. The winters in Shandong were bitterly cold. In the past, people relied on burning charcoal inside the house for warmth, especially at night. It was essential to have charcoal burning beside the bed; otherwise, the bed would be icy cold.

One winter day, as the sunset was fading, Dong Xiasi stoked the charcoal fire, laid out the blankets on his bed, and was about to light the lamp when his friend came to invite him for a drink. So, he locked the door and left with his friend.

The two of them arrived at a small tavern. They sat down and barely had a few drinks before they noticed a crowd gathered around a nearby table, bustling with excitement. They joined the crowd to see what was going on. Turned out that a doctor was sitting there drinking and claiming that he could determine a person's lifespan by taking their pulse. Many people were intrigued and lined up for the doctor to assess their pulses one by one.

Dong Xiasi and his friend also asked the doctor to check their pulse. After taking Dong Xiasi's pulse, the doctor's face showed a surprised expression. He said, "I've had countless people come to me for pulse readings, but I've never seen such an unusual pulse like yours, Mr. Dong! It appears to indicate longevity, yet there are signs of a short lifespan." The surrounding people were surprised and asked for the reasons. The doctor shook his he-

头说道："我的道术也就到这个程度了，不敢妄下结论，董先生今后行事要小心谨慎。"

董遐思刚一听到这话特别害怕，冷静下来后，又觉得这医生的话也不一定是真的，就继续和朋友喝酒聊天，不再胡思乱想。

半夜里，董遐思喝完酒回到家，看见房门虚掩着，他此时有些醉熏熏了，觉得肯定是自己离开时匆忙，没有锁门。

他走进屋里，灯也没开，就准备上床睡觉。他把手伸进被窝里，看看里面暖和了没有，不想却摸到一个滑溜溜的身体。他大吃一惊，缩回了手，急忙点灯查看，竟然看到床上躺着一个漂亮的女子。这女子年轻貌美，肤白如雪，一双丹凤眼妖媚地看着董遐思。她把被子一直盖到脖子的位置，但厚被子也掩盖不住她身体玲珑的曲线。董遐思从来没见过如此美丽的女人，他不禁狂喜，也不问这女人是什么人，就把手伸进被子里，胡乱摸了起来，然而摸到下面的时候，却摸到了一条长长的，毛绒绒的尾巴！他吓得一个翻身就滚到了地上，爬起来正准备跑，美女伸手拽住了董

ad and said, "My skill only goes this far. I do not dare to draw conclusions. Mr. Dong, you should be cautious in your future actions."

Upon hearing these words, Dong Xiasi was initially frightened. After calming down, he thought the doctor's words might not necessarily be true. So, he continued drinking and chatting with his friends, no longer letting his mind conjure up unfounded thoughts.

In the middle of the night, after drinking, Dong Xiasi returned home to find the door slightly ajar. Feeling a bit tipsy, he assumed he must have left it unlocked in haste.

He entered the room, not bothering to turn on the light, and prepared to go to bed. As he reached under the blankets to see if it was warm, he unexpectedly felt a smooth body. Startled, he quickly pulled back his hand and hastily turned on the light to investigate, only to find a beautiful woman lying on the bed. The woman was young and stunning, with skin as white as snow and a pair of captivating eyes fixed on Dong Xiasi. She kept the blankets pulled up to her neck, but even its thickness couldn't conceal her pretty curves. Dong Xiasi had never seen such a beautiful woman before. He couldn't contain his excitement. Without bothering to ask who she was, he reached under the covers and began to touch her all over. However, when his hand reached lower, he felt a long, furry tail! He was so scared that he rolled over and tumbled to the ground. As he scrambled up to get up and run, the woman reache-

遐思的胳膊，问道："你去哪里呀？"

董遐思十分恐惧，他浑身发抖，立刻跪在地上哀求那女妖精饶自己一命。美女笑着说："我不过是一个弱女子，怎么要你的命呀？"说着硬拉着董遐思的手来摸自己，她的大腿肌肤光滑柔软，臀部更是细嫩有弹性，这次董遐思没有摸到尾巴。他连忙道歉，说自己醉得糊里糊涂的，搞错了。但他还是怀疑女子的来历。美女说："你不记得我啦？我家本来住在这东边，后来搬家了，这样算来也是十年前的事情了，那时我还是个小女孩。"

董遐思恍然大悟，说："我好像想起来了，你是周家的阿锁吧？"

美女说："是啊！我就是阿锁！"

董遐思感叹道："没想到十年没见，你出落得如此漂亮！不过，你为什么突然来到我家呢？"

美女说："搬家后不久，我父母就都去世了。我为了活下去，嫁给了一个傻子，过了几年，那傻子和公婆相继去世。现在我成了寡妇，无依无靠，所以来投靠你。"

d out and grabbed Dong Xiasi's arm, asking, "Where are you going?"

Dong Xiasi was very frightened, trembling all over. He knelt immediately and begged the female spirit to spare his life. The woman laughed and said, "I'm just a weak woman. How could I take your life?" She then grabbed Dong Xiasi's hand and made him touch her. Her thighs were smooth and soft, her buttocks tender and elastic. This time, Dong Xiasi didn't feel any tail. He quickly apologized, saying that he was drunk and made a mistake. But he still doubted the woman's identity. The beautiful woman said, "Don't you remember me? My family used to live on the east side here. Then we moved away. Now counting it, it has been ten years since then. Back then, I was just a little girl."

Dong Xiasi had a sudden realization and said, "I think I remember now. You're Asuo from the Zhou family, right?"

The pretty woman replied, "Yes! I am Asuo!"

Dong Xiasi exclaimed, "I never imagined that after ten years, you would become so beautiful! But why did you suddenly come to my house?"

The woman explained, "Not long after we moved, my parents passed away. In order to survive, I married a fool. After a few years, both the fool and my in-laws died. Now I am a widow, with nowhere to turn, so I came to seek refuge with you."

董遐思不再怀疑，他急不可耐地脱了衣服，和美女睡在了一起，夜夜交欢，十分快活。

过了一个多月，董遐思日渐消瘦。家人和朋友们都感觉很奇怪，纷纷让他去看医生。但看了几个医生，都搞不清他到底有什么病。又过了几天，董遐思的面色更加憔悴了，身体也很虚弱，他很害怕，突然想起那天擅长诊脉的医生跟他说的话，他急忙找到那医生。医生给他号了脉，又露出了惊讶的表情："没想到才一个多月不见，董先生的脉象变化如此之大！以前死亡的预兆就要应验了，董先生的病已经没法治了。"

董遐思大哭起来，不肯离开诊所，求医生救自己一命。医生没有办法，只好帮他针灸，又给他开了几副恢复精力的药，并嘱咐他说千万不要行房事。

董遐思回家后，阿锁又嬉笑着挑逗他，要求和他做爱。董遐思把她撵了出去，并生气地说道："你不要再纠缠了，我都快死了！"阿锁忿恨地离开了，走之前她居然说："事到如今，你还想活吗？"

Dong Xiasi no longer doubted her. He eagerly undressed and slept with the beauty. They had sex every night and lived a very happy life.

After more than a month, Dong Xiasi was getting thinner day by day. His family and friends found it strange and they all urged him to see a doctor. But after seeing several doctors, they couldn't figure out what illness he had. A few days later, Dong Xiasi's face was becoming paler, and his body was getting weaker. He was very terrified. Then he suddenly remembered what the doctor who was skilled in pulse diagnosis had told him that day. He hurried to find that doctor. After taking his pulse, the doctor showed a surprised expression again, "I didn't expect Mr. Dong's pulse to change so drastically in just over a month! The signs of death foretold before are about to come true. Mr. Dong's illness is beyond cure."

Dong Xiasi burst into tears, refusing to leave the clinic, and begging the doctor to save his life. The doctor had no choice but to give him acupuncture, prescribe some medicines to restore his energy, and advise him not to engage in sexual activities.

After Dong Xiasi returned home, Asuo teasingly flirted with Dong Xiasi again, demanding to make love. Dong Xiasi kicked her out of the house, angrily saying, "Stop bothering me, I'm about to die!" Asuo left resentfully, but before leaving, she said, "At this point, do you think you can still live?"

到了夜里，董遐思服了汤药，独自一人躺下睡觉。他刚一闭眼就睡着了，梦里他又在和美女阿锁交欢。两人正颠鸾倒凤，如胶似漆时，阿锁的脸慢慢开始变形，她的下巴变尖了，脸上长出了绒毛，最后变成了一张狐狸的脸。原来她是一只狐狸精！这狐狸精卖力地摇晃着腰肢，作势要吸干身下男人的所有精气。

董遐思大叫一声从梦里惊醒，醒来时他发现自己遗精了。他更加害怕，不敢睡觉，让家人点着灯看着他，让他不要睡觉。但一天两天还好，时间长了他怎么能忍得住困意呢？他若一不小心闭上眼睛，就会做同样的梦。就这么过了几天，他又一次在梦里和那狐狸精交欢，醒来后吐了一地的血，然后就一命呜呼了。

本故事改编自《聊斋志异》里的短篇故事《董生》，作者：蒲松龄，生卒年代：公元1610年-1715年。

At night, Dong Xiasi drank the medicine and lay down to sleep alone. As soon as he closed his eyes, he fell asleep. In his dream, he was once again making love with the beautiful woman Asuo. As they were entwined in a passionate embrace and clung to each other like glue, Asuo's face slowly began to transform. Her chin sharpened, fur grew on her face, and finally, it morphed into a fox's face. It turned out she was a fox spirit! The fox spirit vigorously swayed her body, seemingly intending to suck all the vitality from the man beneath her.

Dong Xiasi screamed and woke up from his dream. Upon waking up, he noticed that he had a wet dream, which frightened him even more. Afraid to sleep, he asked his family to keep the light on to watch him, and not let him sleep. However, he could resist not falling asleep for a day or two, but how could he resist for a long time? Whenever he inadvertently closed his eyes, he would have the same dream. After several days like this, he once again had sex with the fox spirit in his dream. Upon waking up, he vomited blood all over the floor. Then took his last breath.

This story is an adaptation of the story *Dong Sheng* from the short story collection *Strange Tales from a Chinese Studio* by Pu Songling (1610 AD to 1715 AD).

【号脉 hào mài】【诊脉 zhěn mài】

号脉或者诊脉是中国传统医学——中医里的一种看病的方法。是通过按触人体不同部位的脉搏，了解病人的病情和病因的一种手段。

Pulse diagnosis, also known as pulse-taking, is a method of diagnosing illnesses in traditional Chinese medicine. It involves assessing a patient's condition and the causes of their illness by feeling the pulse at different points of the body.

【脉象 mài xiàng】

脉象是一个中医学名词，指脉搏的形象与动态，即脉搏的快慢，强弱，深浅的情况。是中医用来判断病人的病情和病因的重要依据。

Pulse condition is a term in traditional Chinese medicine referring to the characteristics and states of the pulse, including its speed, strength, and depth. It serves as an important basis for traditional Chinese medicine practitioners to evaluate a patient's condition and the causes of their illness.

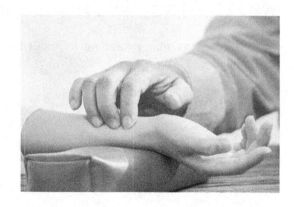

号脉示意图➡

【数不胜数 shǔ bú shèng shǔ】

数不胜数是一个成语。数：计算；胜：尽。放到一起的意思就是：数都数不尽，数都数不过来。形容数量非常多，难以计算。

数不胜数 is an idiom. 数 means to count or calculate. 胜 means exhausted or end. Together this idiom means uncountable or too numerous to count. It is used to describe an extremely large quantity that is difficult to calculate or count.

【丹凤眼 dān fèng yǎn】

丹凤眼是一种眼型：眼睛细又长，但是不小，并且眼尾向上微微翘起来。从古到今，丹凤眼都是中国人认为的好看的眼型。

"Phoenix Eyes" is a type of eye shape: slender and elongated, but not small, with the outer corners slightly raised upwards. From ancient times until now, "Phoenix Eyes" are considered a pretty eye shape in Chinese culture.

【妖精 yāo jing】

妖怪，有魔法或者巫术的鬼神。后面也用来比喻美丽迷人的女子。

Monsters or spirits with magical powers or sorcery. Later, it is also used metaphorically to describe a beautiful and charming woman.

【恍然大悟 huǎng rán dà wù】

恍然大悟是一个成语，意思是忽然一下子明白了，理解了。

恍然大悟 is an idiom meaning to suddenly understand or comprehend something.

【出落 chū luò】

出落是一个动词，指的是青年人，尤其是青年女性的体态和容貌向美好的方面变化。比如："半年没见，邻居家的小姑娘出落得更漂亮了。"意思就是变得更漂亮了。

出落 is a verb describing the change of young people, especially young women, towards a more beautiful appearance and figure. For example: "After half a year without seeing her, the girl from the neighboring house has blossomed even more beautifully." It means she has become prettier.

【急不可耐 jí bù kě nài】

急不可耐是一个成语，意思是：非常着急，都没有耐心，不能等待了。

急不可耐 is an idiom meaning to be extremely eager, lacking patience, and unable to wait.

【交欢 jiāo huān】

动词，意思是：做爱。

It is a verb and it means to make love or have sex.

【房事 fáng shì】

字面的含义是：在房间里发生的事情。指夫妻间性交的事情。上面的交欢是一个动词，而房事是一个名词。比如我们不可以说："你们的交欢怎么样？"但可以说："你们的房事怎么样？"

Literally, it means "things happening in the room." It refers to sexual intercourse between spouses. While 交欢 is a verb, 房事 is a noun. For example, you can't say, "你们的交欢怎么样?" but you can say, "你们的房事怎么样?"

【颠鸾倒凤 diān luán dǎo fèng】

颠鸾倒凤是一个成语，其中"鸾"和"凤"都是指中国传统神话故事中的鸟——凤凰；"颠"和"倒"都是跌倒，倾倒的意思。颠鸾倒凤最开始指的是顺序失常，后来的古代小说里经常用这个词来描述男女交欢。

颠鸾倒凤 is an idiom. 鸾 and 凤 both refer to the mythical bird in Chinese mythology--Phoenix. 颠 and 倒 mean to fall or collapse. 颠鸾倒凤 originally meant disorder or not in the right order, but later in ancient novels it was frequently used to describe sexual activities between men and women.

【如胶似漆 rú jiāo sì qī】

像胶水和油漆那样黏在一起。形容感情炽烈，或者举止亲密，难舍难分。

Like glue and paint sticking together. It describes intense emotions or intimate behavior that is difficult to separate or part from.

【精气 jīng qì】

中医认为，精气是构成人体的基本物质。人如果没了精气，就死了。另外，精这个字可以指"精子"，所以"精气"也可以指男人肾部的活力。如果一个男人纵欲过度，就可以用"精气不足"，"你需要补补精气"这样的话来形容他。

In traditional Chinese medicine, it is believed that 精气 is the basic substance of the human body. If one lacks 精气 (vital energy), they die. Additionally, the character 精 can also be used to mean sperm. So 精气 can also refer to the vigor of the kidneys of men. If a man indulges excessively in sexual pleasures, phrases such as 精气不足 (insufficient vital energy) or 你需要补补精气 (you should eat something to replenish your vital energy) can be used to describe him.

【狐狸精 hú lí jīng】

在中国神话传说中，人可以通过修炼法术变成神仙，或者可以通过在活着的时候多做善事，在死后被封为神仙，比如故事6中的钟馗。也有的人在死后会因为各种原因而变成鬼，比如故事2,4,5里的鬼都是人死了后变的。还有的人会投胎为人或者动物。而动物，可以通过修炼延长自己的寿命，并且还能通过修炼而变化出人的体貌，与人来往。这类动物我们通常称它们为"某某精"，比如狐狸精，耗子精，白蛇精，蜈蚣精，蜘蛛精，等等。其中在民间故事中出现频率最高的就是狐狸精。

In Chinese mythology, people can become immortals through Taoist or Buddhist cultivation or by doing good deeds during their lifetime and being deified after death, like Zhong Kui in story 6. Some people after death may become ghosts for various reasons, like the ghosts in stories 2, 4, and 5. Others may reincarnate as humans or animals. Animals, through cultivation, can extend their lifespan and even change their appearance to that of humans to interact with them. These animals are commonly referred to as "某某精" (something spirit), such as fox spirits, rat spirits, white snake spirits, centipede spirits, spider spirits, and so on. Among these, fox spirits are the most frequently mentioned in folk tales.

狐狸精有公有母，但是最常被提及的还是母的狐狸精。本故事中的狐狸精就是一个传统的狐狸精的形象，她们通过诱惑男人，与他们做爱，吸走男人的精气这种方式来修炼自己的法术，延长自己的寿命。所以狐狸精这个词后来也用来比喻妖媚，爱撒娇，很会勾引男性的女人。

Fox spirits can be male or female, but the most commonly mentioned are female fox spirits. In this story, the fox spirit is a traditional depiction, seducing men and absorbing their vitality through sexual intercourse to cultivate their own magic and extend their lifespan. Therefore, the term "fox spirit" later came to be used metaphorically for a seductive, coquettish woman who is skilled at seducing men.

然而，狐狸精这个形象不是都是邪恶的。在《聊斋志异》中，关于狐狸精的故事有82篇，占全篇故事的20%左右，所以《聊斋志异》又被称为《鬼狐传》。但是在这82篇故事里，有很多狐狸精都是好的形象，它们有的善良真诚，有的机智聪明，有的知恩图报，有的甚至比人类还忠贞不渝。

However, the image of fox spirits isn't always evil. In *Strange Tales from a Chinese Studio*, there are 82 stories about fox spirits, accounting for about 20% of the total stories, so the book is also called *Tales of Ghosts and Foxes*. In these 82 stories, many fox spirits are portrayed positively, some being kind and sincere, some witty and clever, some grateful, and some even more faithful than humans.

除了《聊斋志异》，还有很多古代书籍中也有关于狐狸精的故事。在现代的影视作品里，人们也经常看到这个角色，狐狸精在中国几乎是无人不知无人不晓的形象了。

Besides *Strange Tales from a Chinese Studio*, there are many other ancient books with stories about fox spirits. In modern film and television works, this character is commonly portrayed, resulting in their widespread recognition in China.

【一命呜呼 yí mìng wū hū】

一命呜呼是一个成语，其中，"命"指的是生命，"呜呼"是古代汉语的一个感叹词。一命呜呼的意思就是：死了。它带着一种嘲讽，诙谐的语气。所以我们不能说："我爷爷一命呜呼了"，可以说"那个坏人终于一命呜呼了"。

一命呜呼 is an idiom where 命 refers to life and 呜呼 is an interjection in ancient Chinese. 一命呜呼 means to die. It carries a sarcastic and humorous tone. So, we don't say 我爷爷一命呜呼了 (My grandpa dropped dead.), but we can use it to talk about the death of a villain—那个坏人终于一命呜呼了 (That villain finally bit the dust).

树妖 *The Tree Demon*

本插图由AI Magic Media生成

在秦朝时甘肃省有一个叫做故道的县城。这县城里长着一棵参天大树，枝叶繁密，遮住了周围好几亩地。这些田地因为常年不见阳光，种什么庄稼都不长。当地的村民想要把树砍掉，但是只要拿着斧子靠近大树，天空立刻就雷声大作，电闪雷鸣，暴雨如注。久而久之，人们都认为这棵树肯定已经成精了，不再是一棵普通的树，而是一个树妖了。

新上任的县令得知此事后，决定铲除这个妖怪，派了40个士兵去砍树。士兵们挥动斧头，砍了几十下才把树砍出个小口子，没想到从里面喷出了红色的汁液，像人的鲜血一样，不仅喷涌不断，还带着股难闻的血腥味。更令人吃惊的是，雨水从树干上流到砍坏的口子里，它就像伤口一样迅速愈合了。一些胆大的士兵继续用力砍树，但是情况还像刚才一样。他们砍了一整天，大树依然完好无损。

到了晚上，所有人都很疲惫，回去休息了。只有一个人因为脚受伤而没有回家。他在大树下铺了一个草席，躺了下来，身上盖满了干草。他其实有些害怕不敢睡觉，但是经过这辛苦又惊奇的一天，紧绷的神经在万籁俱寂的夜晚放松了下来，他很快睡着了。

During the Qin Dynasty, there was a town called Gudao in the Gansu province. In the town, there was a towering tree with thick branches and leaves that shaded several acres of land around it. These fields rarely saw sunlight during the year, and so no crops were able to grow. The local villagers wanted to cut down the tree, but as soon as they approached the tree with an axe, the sky immediately rumbled with thunder, flashed lightning, and poured down heavy rain. Over time, people came to believe that the tree must have become a spirit, no longer an ordinary tree, but a tree demon.

The newly assigned magistrate learned about this incident and decided to eliminate this demon. He sent forty soldiers to chop down the tree. The soldiers swung their axes and only made a small dent after multiple times. Unexpectedly, red liquid gushed out from the tree, like human blood. Not only was it gushing out nonstop, but it also carried an unpleasant scent of blood. Even more surprisingly, the rain ran down from the branch and into the opening of the cut, quickly healing and closing like a wound. Some courageous soldiers continued cutting down the tree vigorously. But the same thing happened. After an entire day of effort, the big tree remained perfectly intact.

When night fell, everyone was exhausted and went back to rest. Only one person did not return home due to a foot injury. He laid out a straw mat underneath the big tree, lay down, and covered himself with hay. Frankly, he was a bit scared to sleep. However, after a hard and surprising day, tight muscles finally relaxed under the quiet night. He soon fell asleep.

不知道过了多久，也不知道是做梦还是现实，他隐隐约约地听到有讲话的声音。一个又尖又细的嗓音说道："今天可把你累坏了吧？"

"你少在这幸灾乐祸！"接话的声音有些苍老，但很有底气，像是一个不耐烦的老头儿。

"我哪里有幸灾乐祸，我这不是关心你嘛！我看呀，你这次可是凶多吉少，这县令摆明了要除掉你。"

"他能把我怎么样呢？我再修炼个两百年就成仙了。你这狐狸精想要成仙还早呢，你还是多关心一下你自己吧！"

狐狸精从树上蹦了下来，她尖笑着，好像故意说给树下躺着的士兵听一样："哈哈，要是有人告诉县令，取庙里的香灰来，一边砍你，一边往伤口里撒灰，你个老树妖不就完蛋了？哈哈哈哈哈！"狂笑一顿之后，狐狸精就跑走了，留下树妖在原地气得树枝乱颤，树叶纷纷掉落，飘到士兵的身上和脸上，他一动不敢动，大气都不敢喘，一直挨到天亮。鸡鸣后，他迅速爬起来，跑回去告诉其他人他晚上听到的对话。

Not sure how much time passed, and not sure whether he was dreaming or it was real. He vaguely heard someone talking. A sharp and thin voice said, "Today must have made you feel tired, huh?"

"Quit gloating," the voice that responded had a touch of age but carried authority resembling an annoyed old man.

"I am not gloating. I am worried about you. You see, I think this time you lucked out. The town magistrate obviously wanted to get rid of you."

"What can he do to me? I just need to cultivate for two hundred more years, and I will become a deity. As for you, a fox spirit, it is still too early (for you to become a deity). You should worry about yourself!"

The fox spirit jumped down from the tree, with a sharp laugh, as if purposely saying to the soldier lying underneath the tree, "Ha! If someone tells the town magistrate that by taking the incense ash from the temple and sprinkling it at the wound while cutting you, then you, an old tree demon, would be done for! Ha ha ha!" After laughing wildly for a while, the fox spirit darted away, leaving the tree demon fuming in place with shaking branches and falling leaves. Leaves fell one after another, some fell on the soldier's body and face. He did not dare to move. He didn't even dare to breathe loudly and endured it till daytime. After hearing the roosters crowing, he quickly got up and ran to tell everyone the conversation he heard last night.

士兵们跑遍了附近所有的寺庙，带着香灰回到大树旁，一边砍树一边往砍开的口子里撒香灰，果然血也不流了，那口子也不愈合了。大树终于被拦腰砍断，从里面跳出来一个白头发的老头儿，他身材比普通人高大，力气也很惊人，他用手里的棍子一挥就打倒了一个士兵。其他的士兵们见状，赶紧拿出刀来与之搏斗，厮杀了有半个小时，终于将他杀死。

听说此事的县令赶来查看，但等他抵达时，老头的尸体已经不见了，地上只留下一截粗壮的树根。

本故事改编自《搜神记》，作者干宝（？- 公元336年）

The soldiers ran through all the nearby temples and brought incense ashes next to the big tree. Sprinkling the incense ashes at the cut as they chopped away at the tree. And indeed, the blood stopped flowing out, and the opening no longer closed up. The big tree was finally cut down. An old man with white hair jumped out from the tree. He was bigger than an average person, with incredible strength. With a single swing of the stick in his hand, he swiftly struck down a soldier. When the other soldiers saw the sight, they quickly took out their swords and started fighting. After a fierce battle for roughly half an hour, they finally killed him.

After hearing this incident, the town magistrate quickly came to check. But when he arrived, the old man's corpse had already disappeared, leaving just a thick branch on the ground.

This adaptation is based on a story from *In Search of the Supernatural* by the author Gan Bao (? to 336 AD).

【成精 chéng jīng】 【成仙 chéng xiān】

成精：变成妖精。成仙：变成神仙。

成精: to become a spirit/demon 成仙: to become an immortal; to become a deity/god.

在古人看来，人可以通过修炼而变成神仙，人死后可能会因为各种理由而变成鬼，或者再次投胎。自然界的各种动植物也可以。所以才会有"这辈子做了坏事，下辈子投胎成牛，一生干活受苦"的说法。但不是说只要修炼就一定能变成神仙的，假如修炼的方法不当，可能会变成妖精或者怪物，尤其是动植物，修炼成仙的很少，大多数都变成了某某精，某某妖，或者某某怪，比如这个故事中出现的狐狸精，树妖。

From the perspective of ancient beliefs, people could become immortal or a deity through spiritual cultivation. After death, one could become a ghost for various reasons or reincarnate. The same for all kinds of plants and animals in the natural world. As a result, there is the saying, "If you did bad deeds in your previous life, then in your next life would you become a cow, and endure labor and suffer your entire life." However, not all spiritual cultivation would result in gaining immortality or becoming a deity. If one's cultivation method was improper, one would become a spirit, demon, or monster, especially for plants and animals. Very few of them could become deities. Most became some kind of spirit, demon, or monster—for example, the fox spirit and the tree demon that appeared in this story.

在民间传说故事里，除了少数精怪能够保佑人类，大多数的精怪总是和灾难，干扰和死亡联系在一起。因此，很多故事讲的都是人类如何自己或者在神仙的帮助下除掉精怪。

In folktales and legends, besides a few spirits and monsters that protect humans, most spirits and monsters are linked to disasters, disturbance, and death. Therefore, many stories tell the stories of how humans alone or with the help of gods get rid of spirits and monsters.

另外，成精一词在现代汉语中也经常使用，比如，我们看见一只狗可以用两只后腿走路，还会开门，我们就能惊讶地说："这狗成精了啊！"意思就是，它做出了狗不会做的举动，好像变成更高级的生物了。

Furthermore, 成精 is a frequently used word in modern Chinese. For example, if we see a dog walking backward on its hind legs and even opening a door, we might exclaim in amazement, "This dog has turned into a spirit!" meaning the dog is behaving in a way that is beyond a normal dog as if it has transformed into a higher-level organism.

↑ 古代作品中的狐狸精
本插图选自《聊斋全图》第八册，清光绪时期绘本，现藏于奥地利国家图书馆。

【幸灾乐祸 xìng zāi lè huò】

"幸"的意思是高兴，"乐"的意思是笑，欢乐。幸灾乐祸指的是在别人遇到灾祸时感到高兴。

幸 means happy. 乐 means laughter, joy. 幸灾乐祸 means feeling happy seeing one's unfortunate, or gloating.

【凶多吉少 xiōng duō jí shǎo】

凶：不吉利，不幸。吉：吉利。"凶多吉少"一词用来预测未来，意思是事情可能会向坏的方面发展。

凶: omenious, unlucky, 吉: auspicious. 凶多吉少 is used to predict the future, meaning things are developing in an unfavorable direction.

水鬼

The Water Demon

本插图选自《江乡清夏图》，宋代 刘松年 绘，现藏于台北故宫博物院。

长安城的马镇西宅曾是一位将军的府邸，将军去世后，这宅子已经空置很久，无人居住。相传，将军的后代搬离此处的原因是这宅子里闹鬼。由于多年无人打理，很多房子的屋顶都坍塌了。院子里杂草丛生，一株生命力非常旺盛的藤蔓从凉亭攀爬到了主屋，紧紧掩住了主屋的入口，让本就没有灯光的房间显得更加阴森森了。

有一天，夜幕降临后，在这不知沉寂了几十年的马镇西宅的门前，突然响起了嬉笑的声音。几个少年正手拿着酒壶，坐在门口划拳。其中几个人在长安城小有名气，因为他们都是官宦子弟，父亲或者兄长在朝廷做官，而他们几个经常在私塾下课后，一起喝酒玩乐。

这天晚上，他们决定玩点儿刺激的，喝酒划拳，谁输了谁当天晚上就要住在这个闹鬼的宅子里，其他的人会在宵禁前赶回家里。一番比划之后，只剩下三个人一决胜负了，为了营造氛围，众人决定陪着他们三个人一起走进宅子里，人多胆大，顺便能满足一下所有人的好奇心。

The West Mansion of Ma Town in Chang'an City was once a general's residence. After the general passed away, the mansion had been vacant for a long time with no residents. According to legend, the reason that the general's descendants moved out of the mansion was because it was haunted. Due to so many years of neglect, the roofs of many houses had collapsed. The courtyards were filled with weeds. A vigorously thriving vine climbed from the pavilion to the main house, tightly covering the entrance to the main house, making the rooms that were already without lights even more eerie.

One day, after nightfall, in front of the entrance of the long-dormant West Mansion of Ma Town, which had been silent for decades, laughter suddenly rang out. Several young guys were holding jugs of liquor, sitting at the door playing a drinking game. Some of them were somewhat famous in Chang'an City because they were all children of officials. Their fathers or older brothers held positions in the imperial court. After finishing classes at the private school, they would often gather together to drink and have fun.

This evening, they decided to do something thrilling: drink and play a drinking game. The loser of the game would have to spend the night in this haunted mansion, while the others would rush back home before curfew. After a few rounds, only three remained to compete. To create an atmosphere, everyone decided to accompany the three people into the mansion. With more people came more courage, and it satisfied everyone's curiosity along the way.

走进院子后，他们发现主屋的入口被藤蔓堵死，便决定在凉亭一决胜负，输的人就睡在凉亭里。眼看宵禁时间快到了，三人速战速决，很快分出了胜负，最后输了的人姓韦，是一位协律郎的儿子，我们暂且称他为韦生。说来也巧，韦生平时就自称胆子大，无所畏惧，得此机会，他正好想展示一下自己的胆量，便没有耍赖，欣然留在院子中。其他人跟韦生约好，第二天早上再回到此处相见，随后纷纷离去了。

韦生提着一个灯笼，四处打量这废院。院子里有假山，还有一处池塘，凉亭就在池塘旁边，亭子里石桌石椅一应俱全。韦生嘴上说着不害怕，实际上内心还是有些惴惴不安，为了给自己壮胆，他坐在桌子旁继续喝着朋友们给他留下的酒。酒过三巡后，他躺在地上睡着了。

睡到半夜，他迷迷糊糊地听到有水声，哗啦哗啦的响声唤醒了他的膀胱，他爬起来走到凉亭外面去方便，无意中朝池中一看，水里面好像有什么东西在动。他瞪眼仔细一瞧，月光下，只见水里一个小孩儿冒了出来。小孩儿皮

After entering the courtyard, they found that the entrance to the main house was blocked by vines. So they decided to settle the score in the pavilion. The loser would sleep in the pavilion. Seeing it was soon curfew, the three people swiftly settled their game and declared the result. The person who lost in the end was surnamed Wei. He was the son of an official. For now, we would call him Wei Sheng. Coincidentally, Wei Sheng had always claimed to be brave and fearless. With the opportunity at hand, he wanted to show off his courage. So he didn't renege on the deal and stayed in the courtyard willingly. The others agreed to return here the next morning to meet Wei Sheng. Shortly after, they departed one after another.

Wei Sheng carried a lantern and surveyed the abandoned courtyard. In the courtyard, there were rockeries and even a pond. The pavilion was right beside the pond. The pavilion was fully furnished with stone tables and chairs. Although Wei Sheng claimed that he was not afraid, in actuality, he did feel somewhat uneasy inwardly. To bolster his courage, he sat at the table and continued drinking the liquor left behind by his friends. After three rounds of drinking, he lay down on the ground and fell asleep.

He slept until the middle of the night and was vaguely awakened by the sound of water. The gurgling noise awakened his bladder. He got up and walked outside the pavilion to relieve himself. Inadvertently, he glanced into the pond and it seemed like something was moving in the water. He squinted to take a careful look. Under the moonlight, he saw a child emerging from the water. The child had slightly

肤略黑，身子短腿长，他似乎没有手臂，但还能在水里保持平衡，缓缓地向岸边游来。

韦生见状，赶忙回到凉亭，重新躺了回去，想要装作没有看到。他闭着眼睛，听着水声离自己越来越近，然后是啪嗒啪嗒的小脚步声，那脚步声最后停在凉亭附近。韦生心跳如鼓，正犹豫着要不要睁眼看看时，耳边响起了稚嫩的声音："你是谁？为什么看我？"

韦生翻了个身，从侧卧变成仰卧，但仍旧装睡，不吭一声。小孩儿围着他绕了两圈，停在他的脚边。不一会儿，两只小脚踩在了他的脚上，冰凉的像是冬夜里的冰块儿。韦生还是忍住不动。小孩儿踩着他的小腿向身上走来，一步一步走得很慢，等到那孩子走到韦生的肚子上时，韦生猛地一把抓住他的腿，把他拎了起来。只是等韦生坐起来一看，他抓在手里的居然是一只铁铸的鼎，黑漆漆的非常陈旧，三只鼎脚中已经缺损了一只，只剩下了两只长长的脚。韦生用自己的上衣把它绑在亭子的柱子上。

dark skin and a short body with long legs. He appeared to have no arms, yet could balance himself in the water and slowly swam toward the shore.

Seeing this, Wei Sheng hurriedly returned to the pavilion, lay back down again, and pretended not to have seen anything. He closed his eyes and listened to the sound of the water that was getting closer and closer to him, followed by the pitter-patter sound of small footsteps. The sound of the footsteps eventually stopped near the pavilion. Wei Sheng's heart pounded like a drum as he hesitated whether to open his eyes to take a look. Then next to his ears, a childish voice came through, "Who are you? Why did you look at me?"

Wei Sheng rolled over, changing from lying on his side to lying on his back. However, he still pretended to be asleep and did not say a word. The child circled him twice and stopped at his feet. A moment later, two small feet stepped on his feet. They were cold like winter ice. Wei Sheng held back and remained still. The child stepped on his lower legs and walked up his body, one step at a time, very slowly. When the child reached Wei Sheng's stomach, Wei Sheng suddenly fiercely grabbed his leg and lifted him up. However, when Wei Sheng sat up to take a look, he realized that he was actually holding an iron cauldron, black, extremely old, and worn. One of the three legs was already missing, leaving only two long legs. Wei Sheng tied it to a pillar in the pavilion with his own shirt.

第二天天刚亮，几个朋友就从家里赶来，韦生拿出铁鼎，把自己昨夜的经历详细讲了一遍，众人十分惊奇。他们弄来一把锤子，用力砸向铁鼎，铁鼎碎裂成片，碎片上居然渗出鲜血来。他们更加相信韦生真的碰到了铁鼎精，还降服了铁鼎精，都对他佩服不已。

本故事改编自唐代小说集《玄怪录》，作者牛僧孺（公元780年-848年）。

The next day, just as dawn was breaking, several friends rushed over from their homes. Wei Sheng took out the iron cauldron and told them in detail about his experience last night. Everyone was astonished. They got a hammer and smashed it hard on the iron cauldron. The iron cauldron shattered into pieces, and surprisingly, blood seeped out. They were even more convinced that Wei Sheng had really encountered the iron cauldron demon and defeated it. They were all impressed and admired him greatly.

This story is an adaptation of a story from the Tang Dynasty collection of strange tales *Accounts of Mysteries and Monsters* by author Niu Sengru (780 AD to 848 AD).

【长安 cháng ān】

长安，是现今西安市的古代名称。它是中国历史上建都朝代最多的城市，曾有13个朝代在该城市建立过都城。

长安 (Chang'an) is the ancient name of the modern-day Xi'an City. It is the city with the most number of dynasties in Chinese history, with 13 dynasties having established their capitals in the city.

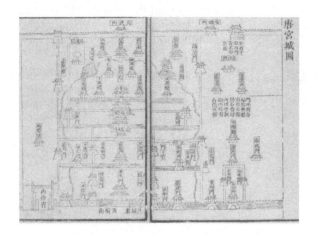

← 古籍中的长安地图

本插图选自《长安志图》，明代西安知府 李氏 刻本，现藏于美国国会图书馆。

【官宦子弟 guān huàn zǐ dì】

"官宦"表示的是做官的人，"子弟"原本指的是儿子和弟弟，后来泛指后代。官宦子弟指的就是官员的孩子们，他们通常家里有钱有势，具有较高的社会地位。这个词用来描述中国旧社会里的一些人更为合适，在现代中国，比较少用到这个词，人们更偏向用"官二代"，"富二代"这样的词来指官员的孩子们和富人的孩子们。

官宦 refers to officials with government positions. 子弟 originally referred to sons and younger brothers, later extending to descendants. 官宦子弟 refers to the children of officials who usually have wealth, power, and high social status. This term is more suitable for describing some people in ancient Chinese society. In modern China, this word is not used frequently. People tend to use words like 官二代 (second generation of an official) or 富二代 (second generation of a rich family) to describe children of officials or wealthy families.

【私塾 sī shú】

在古代由私人设立的教学机构就叫做私塾。

A private educational institution established by individuals in ancient society was called 私塾.

【划拳 huá quán】

划拳是古代人在喝酒时玩的一种游戏。用手，也就是拳头，去比划进行的游戏，所以叫做划拳。在现代中国的一些地区，这个游戏依然活跃在酒桌上。

划拳 is a game that was played by ancient people while drinking. It involves using hands, as in fists, to gesture and compete. Hence the name 划拳. In some regions in modern China, this game is still popular in social drinking settings.

【协律郎 xié lù láng】

协律郎是古代一种官职的名称。

协律郎 is the title of an official position in ancient China.

【一应俱全 yī yīng jù quán】

一应俱全是一个成语。"一应"是一切，"俱"是都，"全"是全部，所有。那么一应俱全的意思就是：应该具备的全都有了。

一应俱全 is a Chinese idiom. 一应 means all things. 俱 means everything. 全 means complete, whole. So the meaning of 一应俱全 is everything necessary has been gathered (complete).

【假山 jiǎ shān】

假山就是假的山，是中式园林中，以造景为目的，用土，石头等材料建的小山。它是中国式庭院建筑的重要组成部分。

假山 means fake mountains. They are little mountains constructed using soil, rocks, and other constructional materials for landscaping purposes in Chinese-style gardens. It is an essential component of traditional Chinese courtyard architecture.

← 该古画中有多座假山

本插图选自《十二月月令图》之一月，清代宫廷画家合作绘制，现藏于台北故宫博物院

【方便 fāng biàn】

方便一词的本意是便利的，省事的。但它也会引申为去上厕所，大小便的意思。"我去方便一下"就是"我去大便"或者"我去小便"的更委婉一些的说法。我们在这里可以看一个有趣的例子：

The word 方便 originally means convenient. However, it can also mean to go to the toilet, either to urinate or defecate. Saying "我去方便一下" is a euphemistic way of saying "I am going to defecate" or "I am going to urinate." Let's take a look at an interesting example here:

一个会讲中文的美国人来中国参加一个会议，在会议上他认识了一些新的朋友，其中一个人是一名记者。这位记者在和他聊天时突然说道："不好意思，我要去方便一下。"他不明白是什么意思，其他人告诉他"方便"就是去上厕所。不久后，记者朋友回来了，继续和美国人交谈，说自己在电视台工作，希望在方便的时候对美国人进行一个采访。美国人十分吃惊地说："怎么能在你方便的时候呢？"那人连忙说："不不！我是说，在你方便的时候。"

An American who could speak Chinese came to China to attend a meeting. During the meeting, he met some new friends. One of them was a journalist. While chatting with him, the journalist suddenly said, "不好意思，我要去方便一下。" (Meaning: Sorry, I need to go to the bathroom.) The American didn't understand what he meant. So the others told him that 方便 meant going to the bathroom. Shortly after, the journalist returned and continued talking to the American. He said that he worked at a television station, hoping to interview the American when 方便 (Meaning: when it is convenient). The American was very surprised and said, "How can you interview me when you are 方便? (Meaning: when you are in the bathroom)" That person quickly clarified, "No, no! I mean, whenever it is convenient for you."

【宵禁 xiāo jìn】

"宵"指的是晚上，"禁"的意思是禁止。宵禁是指在夜间禁止人们出行，所有人必须待在家里的一种制度。在现代社会，通常因为战争或者其它重大事件发生时，政府为了维持社会治安才会采取这种特殊的制度。但是在中国古代社会，宵禁却是一个长期实行的制度，因为在古代，夜间没有照明设施，在夜间出行不仅会受到野兽的攻击，也会因为看不清路而发生意外，统治者为了维护百姓的安全，禁止人们在夜间出行。为了执行这一制度，政府还设定了专门的部门，在夜间巡查，逮捕违反宵禁政策的人们，对他们进行处罚。

宵 refers to night. 禁 means to prohibit. 宵禁 is a system where people are prohibited from going out at night, and everyone must stay at home. In modern society, curfews are usually implemented during times of war or other major events. The government only utilizes this special system when it needs to maintain social order. However, in ancient Chinese society, 宵禁 was a long-standing practice. Because in ancient times, there were no lighting facilities at night. People were not only vulnerable to attacks by wild animals, but also accidents that could happen due to poor visibility. To ensure the safety of people, curfews were imposed to prohibit people from going out at night. To enforce this policy, the government even created a specialized department to patrol at night, apprehend curfew violators, and impose penalties.

【鼎 dǐng】

鼎，中国古代的一种容器，用来煮东西，一般
是由铁或者铜制成的，有三只脚，两只耳朵。

鼎 is an ancient Chinese container used for cooking.
It is typically made of iron or bronze, with three
legs and two ears (handles).

【铁鼎精 tiě dǐng jīng】

在前面两篇故事里，我们看到动物和植物都可以通过修炼变成妖精或
者鬼神。实际上，在中国民间故事中，世界上的万物都可能会变成精
怪，包括物品。因为在中国古代人眼中，无论是人，动物还是植物都
离不开天地和日月的滋养，那么天地和日月一定散发着精华，一种看
不见也摸不着的物质。物品虽然一开始没有生命，但长期在精华的滋
养下，有一天就可能发生变化，变成妖怪。和动物或者植物不同，人
们通常不会认为物品可以成为神仙，而是认为它们会成为妖怪，对人
类没有好处，所以见到它们就一定要消灭它们。

In the previous two stories, we have seen that animals and plants could
become spirits, demons, or gods through spiritual (Taoist) cultivation. In
actuality, in Chinese folklore, everything in the world could potentially become supernatural beings, including objects. Because in the eyes of ancient
Chinese people, whether human, animal, or plant, they couldn't live without
the nourishment provided by heaven, earth, the sun, and the moon. Hence,
heaven, earth, the sun, and the moon must emit essence--an invisible and
intangible substance. Although objects may not have life initially, after being
under the nourishment of essence for a long time, one day they could change
and transform into supernatural beings. Unlike animals or plants, people
generally didn't believe that objects could become deities but rather spirits or
monsters, which were deemed harmful to humans. As a result, they must be
annihilated when encountered.

本故事中的铁鼎精就是由鼎变成的妖怪。虽然不知道它骚扰人类的目
的是什么，但人们认为消灭它总是百利无一害的。

In this story, the iron cauldron demon in this story is a monster transformed from a cauldron. Although it was unclear what its purpose was in disturbing humans, people believed it was always beneficial and would not cause any harm to eliminate it.

故事中关于住宅所用的词汇：

Words related to housing in the story:

【府邸 fǔ dǐ】

在古代，府邸一词指的是贵族，官员或者富人的住宅。在现代社会，通常用来指国家元首，或者身份极其显贵的人的住宅。

In ancient Chinese society, 府邸 referred to the residence of nobles, officials, or wealthy people. In modern society, it usually refers to the residence of the country leaders or people with extremely high status.

↑ 上图照片拍摄的是一位清代皇帝的儿子的府邸正门

本照片选自《醇亲王奕譞及其府邸》，照片约拍摄于1888年，现藏于美国国会图书馆

【宅子 zhái zi】

宅子的意思就是住宅，但通常都指非常大的房子，而且一般不指楼房，指的是那种有院子，房间很多的住所。

宅子 means residence, but it usually refers to a very large house, and usually not just a building, but the kind of dwelling that has yards and a lot of rooms.

【房子 fáng zi 】

泛指所有的人们可以居住或者进行其他活动的建筑物。

refers to all buildings that people can live in or conduct other activities.

【房间 fáng jiān 】【屋子 wū zi】

房间和屋子是近义词，都是指房子里的一个被分隔的组成部分。

房间 and 屋子 are synonyms, both referring to a unit (room) in a house.

勾魂

Soul Snatching

本插图选自《聊斋故事画册》，清代 改琦 绘，现藏于台北故宫博物院。

苏州有个姓余的男人，他很喜欢斗蟋蟀。每到秋天，蟋蟀最多的季节，他就天天带个盆去城外捕捉蟋蟀，黄昏的时候才回家。

有一天，余某回来得晚了一些，城门已经关闭，他着急地徘徊在城门附近，正不知晚上去哪里过夜时，看到两个人向这边走来。其中一个人个子高高的，瘦瘦的，穿着一身白色的衣服，另一个人要更矮一些，也更胖一些，穿着一身黑色的衣服。两个人都背着包袱，看上去像是从外乡来的。

余某好心地走过去对二人说："二位先生，城门关了，不要再往前走啦！今天晚上进不去城了。"

白衣男子笑呵呵地说："谢谢先生提醒，我们不进城，我们住在城东门外，离这里不远。我看先生你应该是耽误了时间，被困在门外了，你若不嫌弃的话，要不来我家借宿一晚？"

余某很高兴，很想答应，但是看到旁边黑衣男子脸色严肃且一言不发，不禁有些犹豫。

In Suzhou, there was a man named Yu, who was very fond of cricket fighting. Every autumn, when crickets were most abundant, he would bring a container and go outside the city to catch crickets every day. Only at dusk did he return home.

One day, Yu returned a bit later than usual, and the city gates were already closed. He anxiously paced near the gate, unsure where to spend the night. Just then, he saw two people walking toward him. One was tall and thin, dressed in white, while the other was shorter and plumper, dressed in black. Both carried bags on their backs and seemed to be from out of town.

Yu kindly approached them and said, "Gentlemen, the city gates are closed. Don't keep walking ahead, as you won't be able to enter the city tonight."

The man in white smiled and said, "Thank you for the warning, sir. We're not entering the city. We live just outside the east gate, not far from here. I see you must have lost track of time and are now locked outside of the gate. If you don't mind, why don't you come stay at our place for the night?"

Yu was pleased and wanted to accept the offer, but when he saw the serious expression on the face of the man in black, who remained silent, he couldn't help but hesitate.

白衣男子看出余某的顾虑，连忙说道："这位是我朋友，姓范。他这个人也很讲义气的，就是不善言辞。"说着，白衣男做了一个请的手势，示意余某一起前行。余某盛情难却，道了谢，就和他们一同向城东走去。路上，余某和白衣男子交谈甚欢，得知白衣男姓谢，朋友们都叫他谢七爷。

走了不久，他们就到了白衣男子家，只见大门敞开着，屋内摆放着很多旧书和一个铜香炉。白衣男让余某在屋里坐着休息，他从外面端来了好酒好菜，三人坐在桌前饮酒吃菜，谈天说地，气氛非常融洽。就连刚才一直黑着脸的范某也露出了笑容。

吃着吃着，余某似乎听到有人在痛苦地呻吟，还有人在哭泣的声音。他问谢七爷这是怎么回事。谢七爷说，邻居家的一位男子已经病入膏肓，活不过今晚了。

余某听后略感忧伤，又多喝了几杯酒，喝得有些醉了，就伏在案上小憩。谢七爷和他的朋友范某仍在一旁喝酒聊天。

The man in white noticed Yu's concern, and he quickly added, "This is my friend, surnamed Fan. He's also a very loyal person, just not good at expressing himself." With that, the man in white made an inviting gesture for Yu to join and go with them. Unable to refuse such hospitality, Yu thanked them and walked with them toward the east gate of the city. Along the way, Yu had a pleasant conversation with the man in white, learning that his name was Xie, and his friends called him Xie Qiye.

They didn't walk long before they arrived at the man in white's house. The door was open, and inside were many old books and a bronze censer. The man in white invited Yu to sit and rest inside while he brought out delicious food and wine from outside. The three of them sat at the table, ate, drank, and chatted about all topics. The atmosphere was very friendly. Even Fan, who had previously been solemn, was now wearing a smile.

As they were eating, Yu seemed to hear someone groaning in pain and even the sound of crying. He asked Xie Qiye what was going on. Xie Qiye explained that a man in the neighboring house was gravely ill and wouldn't survive the night.

Yu felt a bit saddened after hearing this, so he drank a few more drinks. He was becoming somewhat intoxicated, and so he leaned on the table to rest. Xie Qiye and his friend Fan continued drinking and chatting next to him.

夜更深了，谢七爷摇醒睡着的余某，然后从靴子里拿出一张纸，要求余某对着纸哈口气。余某迷惑地看向周围，看见范某不知什么时候穿上了黑色的长袍，还戴了一顶黑色的，高高的帽子，帽子上有四个大字"天下太平"，而谢七爷穿着白色的长袍，戴着白色的高帽，帽子上写着"一见生财"。谢七爷笑着说："余兄帮个忙嘛！对着这张纸哈口气。"余某虽然很迷惑，但因为酒的关系，他还没有十分清醒，也没看清纸上写着什么字，就迷迷糊糊地照办了，他对着纸吹了一口气。忽然，谢范二人变得和屋顶一样高，手指变得又尖又长，像是鸡爪一样。谢七爷的舌头从嘴里垂下来，一直垂到胸部，而范某不知从哪里变出一条铁锁来，眼睛瞪得浑圆，眼神凶恶，他严肃地催促着谢七爷："到时间了！"谢七爷点点头，对吓呆了的余某说："余兄，咱们后会有期，告辞！"说完后，两人走向墙壁，然后就消失不见了。随即听到隔壁哭声骤起，根据人们哀嚎的内容，余某知道是那位病人咽气了。

此刻，余某的酒彻底醒了，他瑟瑟发抖地回顾着刚才发生的事情，突然反应过来，他碰到的这两位就是黑无常范无咎和白无常谢必安啊！他们这是拿着拘捕证

As the night grew deeper, Xie Qiye shook the sleeping Yu awake. Then he took out a piece of paper from his boot and asked Yu to blow on the paper. Yu looked around in confusion and saw that Fan, unknowingly when, had put on a long black robe and was wearing a tall black hat with the words "Peace to the World" written on it. On the other hand, Xie Qiye was wearing a long white robe and a tall white hat. On the hat, the words "Prosperity Upon Sight" were written on it. Xie Qiye said while smiling, "Brother Yu, do me a favor! Blow on this paper." Even though Yu was still confused, because of the alcohol, he was still not fully awake, and he didn't see clearly what the words were on the paper, but he just obeyed anyway. He blew on the paper. Suddenly, Xie and Fan grew as tall as the roof. Their fingers became long and sharp, like chicken claws. Xie Qiye's tongue hung out from his mouth, reaching down to his chest, while Fan produced an iron chain, not knowing from where. His eyes were glaring wide, and had a fierce look. He sternly urged Xie Qiye, "It's time!" Xie Qiye nodded, and said to the stunned Yu, "Brother Yu, we'll meet again. Goodbye!" After saying that, the two walked toward the wall and vanished. Shortly after, cries erupted from the neighboring house. Based on what the people were wailing about, Yu knew that the sick person had passed away.

At that moment, Yu sobered up completely, trembling as he recalled what had just happened. Suddenly, it dawned on him—the two he had encountered were the Black Guard Fan Wujiu and the White Guard Xie Bi'an!

到隔壁家勾魂去了。但是为什么要让自己对着拘捕证吹气呢？是不是自己也快死了呢？

余某越想越怕，就想夺门而出，不过门从外面锁了起来，他拍打着门大喊救命。外面的人听到声音，把锁打开，看见余某以为是小偷，拿起木棍就打。余某连连解释，还把自己捉到的蟋蟀给他们看，这家人里面恰好有认识余某的，余某这才得以脱身。

回到家后，余某每天都心惊胆战，害怕黑白无常来索自己的命。不过，黑白无常没等来，倒是他的运气变好了，他捉的蟋蟀总是会打败对手，让余某赚到了很多钱。就这样，余某一直活到八十多岁。相信他离世的时候，一定再次见到了黑白无常二位勾魂使者了。

本故事改编自清代短篇小说集《子不语》中的一篇故事，作者袁枚（公元1716年-1798年）。

They had come to snatch the soul of the neighbor with the arrest warrant. But why ask him to blow on the arrest warrant? Was his own death near, too?

The more Yu thought about it, the more frightened he became. He wanted to escape through the door, but the door was locked from the outside. He pounded on the door, shouting for help. The people outside heard him and unlocked the door. When they saw Yu, they thought he was a thief and picked up sticks to beat him. Yu tried to explain and even showed them the crickets he had caught. Fortunately, there was someone who knew Yu in the family, and so Yu was able to escape.

After returning home, Yu lived in constant fear every day, dreading the arrival of the Black Guard and the White Guard coming to snatch his soul. However, the two messengers from the underworld did not come. Instead, good luck came to him. The crickets he caught always defeated the opponent, which earned him a lot of money. Just like that, Yu lived to be over eighty years old. It is believed that when he passed away, he once again encountered the two messengers who were responsible for snatching the souls, the Black Guard and the White Guard.

This story is an adaptation of a story from the Qing Dynasty collection of short stories *What Master Confucius Does Not Speak Of*, written by Yuan Mei (1716-1798 AD).

【斗蟋蟀 dòu xī shuài】

斗蟋蟀是中国民间的一种游戏。雄性蟋蟀会为了保卫自己的领地或者争夺配偶而相互撕咬。人们利用蟋蟀这一好斗的特性，将捉到的两只雄性蟋蟀放到一起，让它们互相争斗，而人们在旁边观看，有人还会下注赌博哪只蟋蟀会赢。

Cricket fighting is a popular game in Chinese civil society. Male crickets engage in fights with each other either to defend their territory or to compete for a mate. Taking advantage of this aggressive nature of crickets, people capture two male crickets and put them together to fight while spectators watch on. Some may even place bets on which cricket will win.

【城门 chéng mén】

中国古代的很多城市都建有城墙。修建城墙的主要目的是为了防御敌人进攻。在城市人口增多之后，城墙也具有分割空间的功能，内城通常住着皇帝，高官和富人，外城则住着平民百姓。

In ancient China, many cities had walls built surrounding the city. The primary purpose of building these walls was to defend against enemy attacks. As the population increased in the cities, the walls also served to divide spaces, with the inner city typically inhabited by the emperor, high-ranking officials, and the wealthy, while the outer city housed the common people.

◀ 古代画作中的城市与城墙

本插图选自《水程图》，
明代钱谷、张复 共同绘制
现藏于台北故宫博物院

城门就是指进出城的通道。它通常会在日落之后关闭，并在日出之前开启。这样做也是为了保护城内居民的安全。

The city gates refer to the passages for entering and exiting the city. They would typically be closed after sunset and opened before sunrise. Doing so helped protect the safety of the people living within the city walls.

↑ 古代画作中的城门

本插图选自《金陵图》，清代 谢遂 绘，现藏于台北故宫博物院

【黑白无常 hēi bái wú cháng】

黑白无常是中国民间传说中的一对鬼差。他们负责引导死人的阴魂去往阴间，若是遇见想要逃跑的，或者不想去阴间的鬼魂，黑白无常需要抓住他们，用铁链将逃跑者锁住，强行将其带往阴曹地府。

Hei Bai Wu Chang (The Black Guard and the White Guard) are a pair of underworld officials in Chinese folklore. They are responsible for guiding the souls of the deceased to the underworld. If they encounter souls trying to escape or unwilling to go to the underworld, The Black Guard and the White Guard need to capture them using iron chains and forcibly take them to the underworld.

黑无常，名为范无咎，也被称为"八爷"。他个子较矮，身宽体胖，总是一脸严肃。他身穿黑色的袍子，戴着高高的帽子，上面写着"天下太平"或者"正在捉你"。

The Black Guard (also translated as the Black Impermanence), whose name is Fan Wujiu, is also known as "Lord Eight." He is shorter, broader, and fatter. He always has a serious expression. He wears a black robe and a tall hat with the words "Peace to the World" or "Arresting You Right Now" written on it.

白无常，名为谢必安，人们也称他为"七爷"。他身材高瘦，面色惨白，口吐长舌，时常笑容满面，喜欢恶作剧。他身穿白色袍子，头顶的帽子上写着"一见生财"或者"你可来了"。

The White Guard (also translated as the White Impermanence), whose name is Xie Bi'an, is also known as "Lord Seven." He is tall and thin with a pale complexion and a long tongue hanging out from his mouth. He is often smiling and enjoys mischief. He wears a white robe, and his hat has the words "Prosperity Upon Sight" or "You've Finally Arrived" written on it.

↑ 重庆市丰都鬼城里的黑白无常雕像

本图片由Gwydion M. Williams拍摄，具体版权信息请见本书后面的插图来源

126

据传，人死后，人的灵魂都会见到黑白无常，会被他们带去阴间。所以很多人看到黑白无常就以为自己死了，感到非常恐惧。但也有一些特殊情况，让人在寿命未尽的时候见到黑白无常，单独见到黑无常一般不是好事，因为黑无常除了负责引导阴魂去阴间，还会惩罚活着的坏人。而白无常却可以给人带来发财的好运气，因此有些地方的寺庙里会供奉白无常的神像。

It is said that after death, everyone encounters the Black Guard and the White Guard, who then escort them to the underworld. Therefore, many people, upon seeing the Black Guard and the White Guard, assume they have died and feel extreme fear. However, there are also some special cases where people encounter the Black Guard and the White Guard before their time of death. Meeting the Black Guard alone is generally not a good sign because, besides guiding souls to the underworld, the Black Guard also punishes living evildoers. The White Guard, on the other hand, can bring good luck and wealth. Thus, in some temples, there are statues of The White Guard for people to worship.

【勾魂 gōu hún】

上面说到黑白无常是负责引导死人的阴魂去往阴间的。但他们怎么知道哪个人会死呢？这是因为每个人的寿命是在他出生的时候就定好的，他死亡的时间，地点和方式都被记录在一个叫做生死簿的本子里。等这个人快要死的时候，地府的官员会开出一张拘捕证，交给黑白无常，黑白无常带着拘捕证，在规定的时间到达这个人所在的地方，呼唤他的名字，把他的灵魂从肉体里召唤出来，这个人就死了，黑白无常会带着他的灵魂去地府报到。这个举动就被称之为勾魂。

As mentioned earlier, the Black Guard and the White Guard are responsible for guiding the souls of the deceased to the underworld. But how do they know who is about to die? They know it because each person's lifespan is predetermined at birth. The time, place, and manner of death are recorded in a book called Book of Life and Death. When a person is about to die, officials from the underworld issue a warrant, handing it to the Black Guard and the White Guard. With this warrant, they arrive at the designated location at the appointed time, call out the person's name, summoning their soul from their body, and the person dies. The Black Guard and the White Guard then take the soul to the underworld to report. This action is called soul snatching or soul capturing.

再后来，勾魂一词也用来比喻被某人或某事物所吸引而心神不定。比如："她长着一双勾魂的眼睛"，或者"那个男人呆呆地看着眼前的美女，好像魂被勾走了一样。"

Later on, the term 勾魂 is also used metaphorically to describe being attracted to or captivated by someone or something, causing one's mind to be unsettled. For example, "She has a pair of captivating eyes," or "The man stared blankly at the beautiful woman in front of him as if his soul had been captivated."

【病入膏肓 bìng rù gāo huāng】

病入膏肓是一个成语，其中"膏肓"是古代医学名词，指的是心脏的末端，是那时的医学认为药力达不到的位置，也就是说这个人的病已经到了没有药可以治疗的地步了。这个成语用来表示病情严重到无法治疗，也用来比喻事态严重，无法挽救。

病入膏肓 is an idiom. 膏肓 is an ancient medical term referring to the end part of the heart, which was believed to be beyond the reach of medicine at that time. This means that this person's illness has reached a point where there is no cure. This idiom is used to indicate that the illness is so severe that it is beyond treatment. It is also used metaphorically to describe a serious situation that is irreparable.

鬼吏
Underworld Official

本页插图选自《中山出游图》，元代 龚开 绘，现藏于美国弗利尔美术馆。

汉后元二年，一场可怕的瘟疫袭击了河东郡，无数人被感染，死亡如潮水般蔓延。周式家本来也在河东郡，但是因为父亲在长安获得了一个职位，他们全家搬到了长安，才逃过一劫。周式的几个朋友都在这场瘟疫中去世，周式得知此消息已是3个月后，瘟疫还没有完全退去，他不顾家人的反对，回到河东郡去寻找他失去联系的好友。只可惜，等他赶到好友家时，发现他已经被病毒夺走了生命，为了防止感染，连葬礼也没办，就被草草地下葬了。

周式只好伤心地离开，为了尽量减少被感染的可能性，他没有走陆路，而是包了一艘小船，顺着黄河而上，向长安方向驶去。船出发了大约十多里地时，周式看到岸边一个人在对着船招手。通常这样的人都是希望能搭个便船。但最近由于病毒肆虐，很多人都不愿让陌生人上船。然而此刻，周式正试图从好友离世的忧伤情绪中脱离出来，他命船夫把船停靠岸边，让陌生人上了船。此人自称姓牛，是一个官吏，要去京城办事，他租的船出了故障无法前行，只好在岸边碰运气，看有没有人愿意让他搭船，但人们恐惧瘟疫不敢让他上船，他站

In the Second Year of Houyuan in the Han Dynasty, a terrible plague struck Hedong Province, infecting countless people, and death spread like a tide. The Zhou family originally lived in Hedong Province, but because his father obtained a position in Chang'an, their entire family moved to Chang'an, therefore narrowly escaping the disaster. Several of Zhou Shi's friends passed away in this plague. It was three months later when Zhou Shi learned of this news. At that time, the plague had not completely subsided. Despite his family's opposition, he returned to Hedong Province to find his friend with whom he had lost contact. Unfortunately, when he arrived at his friend's house, he found that he had already been taken by the virus. To prevent infection, his friend was hastily buried without a funeral.

Zhou Shi had no choice but to leave with sorrow. To minimize the possibility of infection, he did not travel by land. Instead, he rented a small boat, sailing upstream along the Yellow River toward Chang'an. When the boat had traveled about ten kilometers, Zhou Shi saw a person waving at the boat from the shore. Usually, such people hoped to hitch a ride. But recently, due to the rampant virus, many people were unwilling to let strangers board their boats. However, at this moment, Zhou Shi was trying to break free from the sadness of his friend's death. He ordered the boatman to dock by the shore and let the stranger board the boat. The man said his last name was Niu, a government official who was going to the capital to handle official matters. The boat he rented had broken down and couldn't move forward. So, he had no choice but to try his luck on the shore to see if any-

了很久才搭上周式的船，对周式感激不已。

周式和这官吏攀谈起来，发现他去过很多地方，周式对他的各地见闻很感兴趣，俩人一直聊天到深夜，直到官吏哈欠不断，才熄灯睡觉。睡觉前，官吏指着他随身携带的一卷文书说："这卷文书是机密，我睡着后，你千万不要打开它。"周式连声答应，二人相继沉沉地睡去。

第二天一早，周式早早醒来，那官吏还在睡着。周式看到包裹文书的布料不知什么时候散开了，隐约看到文书上写着三个字"姓名簿"。他实在忍不住好奇心，就悄悄地打开文书偷阅。文书上面写着很多名字，名字的旁边有具体的死亡时间和死亡理由，他看到了他好朋友的名字以及死亡原因"瘟疫"。他纳闷地往下翻阅，赫然看到自己的名字，死亡时间是两天后，还没等看到死亡理由，手里的文书被一把夺走。那官吏生气地说："我特别交代过你，你竟然不当一回事！天机不可泄露，你死后到阴司报道时可

one would be willing to let him hitch a ride. But people, fearing the plague, did not dare to let him board their boats. He stood for a long time before finally boarding Zhou Shi's boat, and he was immensely grateful to Zhou Shi.

Zhou Shi and the official began chatting, and Zhou Shi learned that the official had traveled to many places. Zhou Shi was very interested in what he had seen and heard in different places. The two of them chatted until late into the night, only stopping when the official couldn't stop yawning, and so it was time to turn off the light and sleep. Before going to sleep, the official pointed to a scroll he carried with him and said, "This scroll is confidential. After I fall asleep, you must not open it." Zhou Shi repeatedly promised not to open it, and both fell into deep sleep.

The next morning, Zhou Shi woke up early, and the official was still asleep. Zhou Shi noticed that the cloth wrapping the scroll had come loose at some point, and he glimpsed three characters written on the scroll: "List of Names." He couldn't resist his curiosity, so, he stealthily opened the scroll to peek. On the scroll, many names were written on it. Next to the names were specific dates of death and causes of death. He saw his good friend's name and the cause of death: "plague." Perplexed, he continued reading and was shocked to see his own name, with the death date being two days later. Before he could read the cause of death, the scroll was snatched away from his hands. The official said furiously, "I specifically instructed you, yet you disregarded it! The divine plan must not be revealed to humans.

千万不要说你看过这文书，不然我可是会受到责罚的！"

周式听了这话才明白这人不是普通的官吏，而是一个鬼吏，是按照这名单上的名字来索命的。他赶紧跪下不停地磕头，求鬼吏饶自己一命。过了很久，鬼吏无奈说道："你让我搭船这么远，我应该感谢你，但是这文书我是改不了的，我告诉你一个方法，下船后你赶紧回家，三年内都不要出门，就可以免于一死。不要对任何人提起你见过我或者文书的事情。否则我就帮不了你了。"

周式回家后，无论昼夜都没有踏出门口一步。一开始，家人以为他是因为众多好友去世而心情忧郁，所以没有强迫他出门。后来，家人们又觉得他得了什么疾病，叫来很多医生来家里看病，都没看出来有什么问题，而周式这次履行了承诺没有向任何人提起鬼吏的事情。就这样过了两年多，周式一直待在房间里，身体当然变得虚弱了，他的父母非常担心。有一天清晨，趁着周式没睡醒，他们找了几个壮汉，把周式抬到了离家一条街远的医馆里去诊病。周式醒来发现自己身处陌生的地方，吓得跳起来想要赶紧跑回家，结果刚出门就碰到了

When you report to the underworld after your death, you must not mention that you've seen this scroll, or I will be punished!"

After hearing these words, Zhou Shi realized then that this person was no ordinary official but rather an underworld official who claimed lives according to the names on that list. He quickly knelt and kowtowed repeatedly, begging the underworld official to spare his life. After a long while, the underworld official, with no other choice, said, "You gave me a ride and brought me this far, I should thank you. But I cannot alter this scroll. I'll tell you a way. After you get off the boat, hurry back home, and do not go outside for three years. Then you'll avoid death. Do not mention to anyone that you have seen me or the scroll. Otherwise, I can't help you."

After returning home, Zhou Shi never stepped out of his house, day or night. At first, his family thought he was grieving over the deaths of many friends, so they didn't force him to go out. Later, they thought he had some illness and called many doctors to diagnose him, but they did not find any problem. Zhou Shi kept his promise this time and didn't mention the underworld official to anyone. More than two years passed like that, Zhou Shi stayed in his room all the time, and naturally, his health deteriorated. His parents were very worried. One early morning, while Zhou Shi was still asleep, his parents found several strong men and had them carry Zhou Shi to a clinic a street away from home to be examined. When Zhou Shi woke up, he found himself in a strange place, and in fear, he jumped up and tried to run back home hastily. However, as soon as he stepped out of the door, he

那个鬼吏。鬼吏说："我让你三年内不要出门，你怎么不听呢？你如果不出门的话，就不会被太阳和月亮捕捉到你的精气，我也就找不到你。但现在既然找到了你，我也没有办法，三天后的中午，我会来取你的命。"说完就消失不见了。

周式哭着回到家，对家人诉说了此事，埋怨他们硬把自己抬出了家门。他的父亲不相信他的话，而是认为他果然得了精神病了。他的母亲和其他家人则日夜守护着他，到了三天后的中午，在所有家人的陪伴下，周式突然对着空气大喊："饶我一命吧！"然后就摔倒在地上，死了。

本故事改编自《搜神记》，作者干宝（？ - 公元336年）

ran into the underworld official. The underworld official said, "I told you not to leave your home for three years. Why didn't you listen? If you hadn't left, the sun and the moon wouldn't have captured your vital energy, and I wouldn't have found you. But now that I've found you, I have no choice. At noon, after three days, I'll come to take your life." With that, the underworld official disappeared.

Zhou Shi returned home crying and told his family about the incident, blaming them for forcibly taking him out of the house. His father didn't believe his words. Instead, his father thought that he had indeed gone mad. His mother and other family members guarded him day and night. Three days later, at noon, with all his family members present, Zhou Shi suddenly shouted to the air, "Spare my life!" then collapsed to the ground, and died.

This story is adapted from *Anecdotes About Spirits and Immortals* by author Gan Bao (? - 336 AD).

【汉后元二年 hàn hòu yuán èr nián】

在中国封建社会，不用公元来记录年份，而是使用一种叫做年号的方式来记录年份。年号就是年的名称，通常为两个字，也有少数情况会有三个字甚至四个字，这个名称一般由皇帝决定。本故事中的"后元二年"就是汉代时期的一位皇帝的年号，换算成公元纪年，约为公元前142年。

In the Chinese feudal society, the Gregorian calendar was not used to record years, instead, a system called "nianhao" was used to record years. "Nianhao" (era name) was the name of the year, typically consisting of two characters, although there were rare instances of three or even four characters. The name was usually determined by the emperor. In this story, "Second Year of Houyuan" was the "nianhao" used by an emperor during the Han Dynasty. When converted to the Gregorian calendar, it would be the year 142 BC.

【河东郡 hé dōng jùn】

河东郡是汉代时期的地名，地处范围大约在现今山西省的南部。

河东郡 was a geographical name during the Han Dynasty, located roughly in the southern part of present-day Shanxi Province.

↑ 16世纪一张中国地图上的河东郡所在位置

本插图选自《天下舆地图》，明代时期绘制，现藏于法国国家图书馆

【长安 cháng ān】

长安，是现今西安市的古代名称。它是中国历史上建都朝代最多的城市，曾有13个朝代在该城市建立过都城。

Chang'an was the ancient name of present-day Xi'an city. It served as the capital for more dynasties than any other city in Chinese history. Thirteen dynasties established their capitals in this city.

【黄河 huáng hé】

黄河发源于青藏高原，从西向东横穿中国，总长约为5464公里，是中国最重要的河流之一。黄河流域是中华文明最主要的发源地，因此中国人称黄河为"母亲河"。

The Yellow River originates from the Qinghai-Tibet Plateau and flows across China from west to east, with a total length of approximately 5,464 kilometers. It is one of the most important rivers in China. The Yellow River basin is the primary origin of Chinese civilization, hence the Chinese people refer to the Yellow River as the "Mother River."

↑ 古画中的黄河和船只

本插图选自《乾隆南巡图卷》第四卷，清代 徐扬 绘，现藏于大都会艺术博物馆

【天机不可泄露 tiān jī bù kě xiè lòu】

天机不可泄露是一个成语。在中国古代，人们认为世界上的所有事情都是上天安排好的，包括人的生老病死。这些安排都是上天的机密，事先不能泄露，否则会有不好的后果。

天机不可泄露 is a Chinese idiom. In ancient China, people believed that everything in the world was arranged by the gods living in heaven, including people's birth, aging, illness, and death. These arrangements were considered secrets of heaven and should not be revealed in advance, otherwise, there could be adverse consequences.

【官吏 guān lì】

官吏是古代时政府工作人员的总称。

官吏 was the general term for government officials in ancient times.

【鬼吏 guǐ lì】

鬼吏是指为阴间政府工作的官吏。关于阴间的解释请看故事5后面的关键词。

鬼吏 refers to officials who work for the underworld government. For more explanation on the underworld, please refer to the keywords in story 5.

亡儿托梦

Deceased Son Visits in Dream

本图片由AI生成

在三国时期，有一个将军叫蒋济，是著名历史人物曹操的心腹谋士，他是一个英勇，聪明并且忠诚的人。史书上记载蒋济有一个儿子叫蒋秀，在蒋济死后继承了他的爵位。但我们今天要讲的不是关于蒋秀，而是蒋济的另一个儿子的故事。

During the Three Kingdoms period, there was a general named Jiang Ji, who was a trusted advisor to the famous historical figure Cao Cao. He was a brave, intelligent, and loyal man. Historical records mention that Jiang Ji had a son named Jiang Xiu, who inherited the peerage after Jiang Ji's death. But today we're not talking about Jiang Xiu, instead, we will tell the story of Jiang Ji's other son.

蒋济的另一个儿子叫什么名字，什么时候死的，以及死亡原因，史书上都没有记录，但根据民间传闻，这个儿子是英年早逝。我们接下来就以"蒋儿"来称呼他。

The name, time of death, and cause of death of Jiang Ji's other son are not recorded in historical records. However, according to folklore, this son passed away at a young age. In the following, we'll refer to him as "Jiang Er."

蒋儿死后，他的母亲经常以泪洗面，非常思念蒋儿。有一天晚上，蒋儿的母亲梦见了死去的儿子，他看起来很疲惫，身型消瘦，哭着跪在母亲面前，让母亲救救他。随后，他具体讲述了他在阴间受的苦难。原来，他死后本应该是等着投胎，但因为他是将军的儿子，阴司觉得他有才能，就把他留在阴间工作，指派给泰山府君。但现任泰山府君不是很赏识他，就让他做了最低等的差役。蒋儿生前是将军的儿子，生活舒适富足，不仅没做过如此辛苦的差事，也没像这样受过其他人的轻怠。

After Jiang Er's death, his mother's face was often streaked with tears as she missed him dearly. One night, Jiang Er's mother dreamed of her deceased son. He appeared tired and thin, kneeling before her, crying and pleading for her to save him. He went on to describe the suffering he endured in the underworld. It turned out that after his death, he was supposed to be waiting for his reincarnation. However, because he was the son of a general, the underworld government deemed him talented and retained him to work in the underworld. He was assigned to work under the Lord of Mount Tai. However, the current Lord of Mount Tai did not appreciate him much and placed him in the lowest-ranking position. Jiang Er, when he was alive as the son of a general, lived a comfortable and prosperous life. Not only had he never done such a menial task before, but he had never been treated with such disdain by others.

他母亲听到儿子的哭诉倍感心痛，但她明白生死不同路，阳间的将军无法支配阴间的士兵。蒋儿又说："我这次能来母亲的梦里，是因为我奉命来接新的泰山府君，他叫孙阿，住在太庙的西边。请母亲替我禀告父亲，让他拜托孙阿把我调到舒服的地方去。"

听完这些话，蒋儿的母亲忽然惊醒了，她慌忙叫醒蒋济，并把梦里的事情告诉给他。但蒋济却说："日有所思，夜有所梦，你这是太过思念亡儿而产生了幻觉。梦里的事情都是虚假的。"

蒋济的妻子见她无法说服蒋济，感到非常难过与不安。到了晚上，她又梦见儿子，他说："母亲，今晚是我在人间停留的最后一晚，因为新泰山府君明天中午就会从人间离世，去往阴间赴任，而我也要随他而去，不知什么时候才能回来了，儿在此与母亲拜别。我知道父亲不信鬼神之事，但还是求母亲再次禀告父亲，反正也没有损失，为什么不抱着怜惜儿的心情，去试一下呢？"之后，他详细描述了孙阿住的地方，孙阿的家境和长相。

His mother's heart ached deeply upon hearing her son's lament, but she understood that the living and the dead walked different paths, and a general in the mortal realm could not control the soldiers in the underworld. Jiang Er then said, "I can appear in your dream this time because I've been tasked to welcome the new Lord of Mount Tai, named Sun E, who resides west of the Imperial Ancestral Temple. Please inform Father to ask Sun E to transfer me to a more comfortable position."

Upon hearing these words, Jiang Er's mother suddenly woke up. She hurriedly woke Jiang Ji and recounted the dream to him. However, Jiang Ji said, "One's thoughts by day shape one's dreams by night. Your excessive longing for our departed son has conjured up this illusion. What happened in your dream is not real."

Jiang Ji's wife, unable to convince him, felt very sad and uneasy. The following night, she dreamed of her son again. He said, "Mother, tonight is my last night in the mortal realm because the new Lord of Mount Tai will pass away in the mortal realm tomorrow at noon and depart for the underworld to assume his new position in the underworld. I must accompany him, and I don't know when I'll return. I bid you farewell, Mother. I know Father doesn't believe in ghosts or spirits, but I implore you to plead with him once more. There's no harm in trying, so why not approach him with your empathy for me and give it a try?" Then, he described Sun E's residence in detail, including his family situation and physical appearance.

天亮后，蒋济的妻子再次请求蒋济，这次，蒋济派人去梦里听到的地方去寻找孙阿，果然找到了，他的长相和家境与梦里蒋儿说的一模一样。蒋济立刻召见了孙阿，把妻子梦到的事情告诉他，并承诺若是孙阿帮了蒋儿，蒋济不仅会给他丰厚的赏赐，还会在孙阿去往阴间后，帮他照顾他在人间的家人。

孙阿身体非常强壮，不能相信自己一会儿就会死，他将信将疑地说："如果真的像您说的那样，我当然愿意帮助您的儿子，不知要派您儿子做个什么职务呢？"

蒋济说："就按照他自己所愿，找个轻松快乐的差事给他做吧。"

孙阿答应了下来，然后拿着赏赐回家了。蒋济派人去孙阿家门口守着，想要知道他是否如梦里蒋儿所说，会在当日中午去世。

不久后，传来消息说，孙阿在家吃饭时突然胸口痛，还没等医生赶到就倒地死了。蒋济和妻子泪流满面，蒋济感叹到："虽然我儿不幸早逝，让我伤心不已，但他死后的事情我能知道，还能帮上忙，这也让我感到释然了。"

At dawn, Jiang Ji's wife once again pleaded with him. This time, Jiang Ji sent someone to the place described in the dream to find Sun E. Indeed, they found him. His physical appearance and family situation were exactly as Jiang Er had described in the dream. Jiang Ji immediately summoned Sun E, told him of his wife's dream, and promised that if Sun E helped Jiang Er, he would not only reward him handsomely but also take care of Sun E's family in the mortal realm after his departure to the underworld.

Sun E was strong and healthy, so he couldn't believe his imminent death. He said skeptically, "If what you say is true, of course, I am willing to help your son. What position should I assign him to?"

Jiang Ji said, "Let's follow his wish, and find him an easy and joyful position."

Sun E agreed and returned home with the reward. Jiang Ji sent someone to wait outside Sun E's house, wanting to know if he would indeed die as Jiang Er had said in the dream, at noon that very day.

Shortly after, news arrived that while Sun E was having his meal at home, he suddenly felt chest pain and collapsed before the doctor could arrive. Jiang Ji and his wife were in tears. Jiang Ji lamented, "Although my son's untimely death saddens me deeply, being able to know what happened to him after his death and being able to help him brings me solace."

又过了一个多月，蒋儿再次托梦给母亲说："母亲，我已经被调任了。"说完这句话，他就急匆匆地离开了。

本故事改编自《搜神记》，作者干宝（？ - 公元336年）

Over a month later, Jiang Er appeared in his mother's dream again, saying, "Mother, I've been transferred." With these words, he hurriedly departed.

This story is adapted from *Anecdotes About Spirits and Immortals* by author Gan Bao (? - 336 AD).

【三国 sān guó】

三国是中国的一个历史时期，具体为公元220年至280年。在该历史时期里诞生了很多著名的历史人物，如曹操，孙权，诸葛亮等。中国四大名著之一的《三国演义》就是写的这个时期发生的故事。

The Three Kingdoms was a historical period in China that spanned from 220 AD to 280 AD. During this period, many famous historical figures were born, such as Cao Cao, Sun Quan, and Zhuge Liang, etc. The novel Romance of the Three Kingdoms, one of the Four Great Classical Novels of Chinese literature, tells the stories that occurred in this period.

【曹操 cáo cāo】

曹操是三国时期的一位重要的历史人物。他是中国历史上杰出的政治家，军事家，文学家和书法家。历史上有很多关于他的文学和戏曲作品。在现代中国，也有很多影视剧作品中可以看到曹操这个人物形象。在中国，曹操几乎是一个家喻户晓的历史人物。

Cao Cao was an important historical figure during the Three Kingdoms period. He was an outstanding politician, military strategist, writer, and calligrapher in Chinese history. There are many literary and dramatic works about him throughout history. In modern China, Cao Cao's character can be seen in many film and television productions. In China, Cao Cao is pretty much a historical figure known to everyone.

【谋士 móu shì】

谋士，是指出谋划策的人，在古代的战争时期，谋士这个职业非常兴旺。谋士通常负责出主意，但不负责执行。

谋士 refers to someone who plans and strategizes. During ancient warfare, the strategist profession was very popular. Strategists were usually responsible for coming up with ideas but not responsible for executing them.

【英年早逝 yīng nián zǎo shì】

英年早逝是一个成语，意思是在青壮年时期就早早地去世了。

英年早逝 is an idiom. It means to pass away at a young age or in one's prime.

【泰山府君 tài shān fǔ jūn】

泰山府君，又称太山府君，泰山王，是中国神话体系中的一个职位，负责治理鬼魂。在民间传说里，泰山府君由正直的人担任，五百年一更换。

泰山府君, also known as 太山府君 or 泰山王, is a position in the Chinese mythological system responsible for governing ghosts. In folk legends, the Lord of Mount Tai is held by a righteous person and changes every five hundred years.

【太庙 tài miào】

太庙又称为皇帝的"宗庙"，是古代皇帝祭祀祖先的地方。太庙内供奉着本朝皇帝的神位，从开国皇帝到现任皇帝。但是如果朝代灭亡了，那么新朝代的皇帝会焚毁前朝的太庙，因此现今留下的太庙寥寥无几。目前，可以被大众参观的太庙在北京，始建于1420年，是明清两代皇帝祭祖的地方。

The Imperial Ancestral Temple, also known as the Emperor's Ancestral Temple, was where ancient emperors held ceremonies honoring their ancestors. The Imperial Ancestral Temple enshrines the ancestral tablets of emperors from the founding emperor to the current reigning emperor. However, if a dynasty fell, the emperor of the new dynasty would destroy the ancestral temple of the previous dynasty. Therefore, there are very few Imperial Ancestral Temples remaining today. Currently, the Imperial Ancestral Temple that the public can visit is located in Beijing, built in 1420, and was the place where the emperors of the Ming and Qing dynasties held ceremonies honoring their ancestors.

【禀告 bǐng gào】

禀告的意思是下级向上级报告，在古代汉语中使用较多，用来表达对上级的尊敬。在现代汉语中，已经不太使用这个词了。

禀告 means to inform or report from a subordinate to a superior. It was commonly used in ancient Chinese to express respect for superiors. In modern Chinese, this term is not really being used.

【赏赐 shǎng cì】

赏赐也是中国古代常用的词语，表示地位高的人把财物送给地位低的人，既是动词也是名词，比如："皇帝赏赐给我一百两黄金"，"这是皇帝给你的赏赐"。

赏赐, a term commonly used in ancient China. It means a person of high status giving money or goods to a person of lower status. It is both a verb and a noun. For example, "The emperor bestowed upon me one hundred taels of gold" or "This is the reward given to you by the emperor."

【托梦 tuō mèng】

在道教和中国民间信仰中，鬼和人是无法直接沟通的，除非和一些有特殊能力的人，比如像会法术的道士等。那么鬼如果想要和人交流，是可以出现在这个人的梦里，然后和这个人对话的。比如在本故事中，蒋儿多次出现在母亲的梦里，跟她沟通，这种死人去到活人梦里的现象就叫托梦。

In Taoism and Chinese folk beliefs, ghosts and humans cannot communicate directly except with certain individuals with special abilities, such as Taoist monks with spiritual power. Therefore, if a ghost wants to communicate with a person, it can appear in that person's dreams and have a conversation with them. For example, in this story, Jiang Er appeared in his mother's dreams multiple times to communicate with her. This phenomenon of the deceased visiting in the dreams of the living is called 托梦.

附身

Body Possession

本页插图选自《聊斋全图》第十一册，清光绪时期绘本，现藏于奥地利国家图书馆。

在清朝时，常州有一个叫做李化的人，家中有很多块田地，是当地有名的富人。虽然那时候很多官员和富人都会娶多个女人做老婆，李化却只娶了一位妻子。他们夫妻二人感情恩爱，但可惜只有一个女儿，她叫小惠，容貌秀美，温柔可人，夫妻俩非常疼爱她。不想世事难料，小惠十四岁时得了暴病，突然死了，家里顿时冷清起来。夫妇二人还想再生个小孩，可是李化已经五十多岁，他夫人也四十多了。于是，李化娶了个小老婆。两年过后，小老婆给他生了个儿子，全家人视这个孩子为珠宝一般，给他取名叫珠儿。

珠儿渐渐长大，个头比同龄人高，也比同龄人强壮，但是脑子有些痴呆，已经五六岁了还讲不清楚话，甚至分不清哪些东西能吃，哪些东西不能吃。李化照样疼爱他，不在乎他的毛病。有一天，李化带着珠儿去逛集市，碰到个独眼僧人，这僧人拦住李化说他能掌握人的生死祸福，要求李化给他一百两银子，若是不给，李化这唯一的儿子就会夭折。

During the Qing Dynasty, there was a man named Li Hua in Changzhou. He owned many fields and was a well-known wealthy man in the area. Although it was common for many officials and wealthy men to have multiple wives at that time, Li Hua had only one wife. The couple had a loving relationship but unfortunately only had one daughter, named Xiaohui. She was beautiful and gentle, and her parents adored her very much. However, life's unpredictability struck when Xiaohui was fourteen years old. She fell seriously ill and suddenly died, leaving the household in a state of instant desolation. The couple wanted to have another child, but Li Hua was already over fifty, and his wife was in her forties. So, Li Hua had taken in a second wife. Two years later, the second wife gave birth to a son. The whole family cherished the child like a precious gem and so they named him Zhu'er.

As Zhu'er gradually grew up, he was taller and stronger than his peers but somewhat mentally challenged. At five or six years old, he still couldn't speak clearly and couldn't distinguish between what was edible and what wasn't. Despite these issues, Li Hua loved him dearly and did not mind his problems. One day, Li Hua took Zhu'er with him to the market, and they encountered a one-eyed monk. The monk stopped Li Hua and said he could control people's lives and luck. He demanded a hundred taels of silver from Li Hua. If he didn't pay, Li Hua's only son would die prematurely.

李化不相信这等迷信说法，没有给僧人钱财。几天后，珠儿突发恶疾，不治身亡。李化非常悲恸，向县令告状，县令派人拘捕了独眼僧人，搜了他的身，在他身上发现了两个小木人，一个小棺材和一些符咒。僧人刚开始不承认自己做法害了珠儿，但符咒上的文字已经显示了他的恶行。县令命令手下对其严刑拷打，最终，僧人承认自己下了诅咒害了珠儿的性命，还说即便他不下诅咒，珠儿也是夭折的命，他不过是将珠儿的死期提前了一点而已。县令听到僧人的狡辩非常愤怒，命令手下将僧人处死。

僧人死后，李化谢过县令就回家了。他躲开妻子，一个人躺在床上，非常悔恨自己过于固执，假若他能抱着破财免灾的想法，珠儿现在或许还能活着。他悲痛欲绝，忍不住放声大哭。哭着哭着忽然听到一个小孩子的声音："阿爸，不要太难过了。"李化吃了一惊，赶忙坐起来，看到床边站着一个七八岁的小男孩，他若隐若现，恍恍惚惚地像烟雾一样。他爬上了床，坐在李化旁边。李化吓得伸手推他，小孩儿掉到了地上，但是他掉地时一点儿声音都没有。被推到地上他也没哭，而

Li Hua didn't believe in such superstitions and did not give the monk any money. A few days later, Zhu'er suddenly caught a vicious disease that couldn't be cured and died. Li Hua was grief-stricken. He reported the incident to the county magistrate. The county magistrate dispatched officers to arrest the one-eyed monk. They searched him and found two small wooden figures, a small coffin, and some talismans on the monk. Initially, the monk denied casting curses to cause Zhu'er harm, but the writings on the talismans revealed his malicious actions. The county magistrate ordered his subordinates to torture the monk severely. In the end, the monk confessed to placing a curse that killed Zhu'er. He also claimed that even without the curse, Zhu'er was destined to die young, and he had merely hastened his death slightly. Enraged by the monk's excuses, the county magistrate ordered his men to execute him.

After the monk's death, Li Hua thanked the county magistrate and returned home. Avoiding his wife, he lay alone on the bed, deeply regretting his stubbornness. If only he had embraced the idea of "spending money to prevent misfortunes," Zhu'er might still be alive. Overwhelmed by grief, he could no longer restrain himself and began crying loudly. While crying, he suddenly heard a child's voice, "Dad, don't be too sad." Startled, Li Hua sat up quickly and saw a boy around seven or eight years old standing by the bed. He appeared and disappeared intermittently, hazy like smoke. The boy climbed onto the bed and sat next to Li Hua. Frightened, Li Hua reached out to push him away, and the boy fell to the floor, but there was no sound at all when he landed.

是淡定地爬起来对李化说："阿爸，干嘛这样呢？"说完又爬上了床。

李化害怕地逃出了房间，躲进妻子所在的房间里，把那小孩儿关在了门外。可是他回头一看，小孩儿已经站在他腿边了。他声音颤抖地问那小孩儿到底想干什么，为什么叫自己为阿爸。小孩儿回答说："我是苏州人，姓詹，六岁时在家门口玩耍，被妖僧带走杀死，埋在一棵桑树底下，之后他就用法术控制我的阴魂，让我帮他一起害人。幸亏阿爸你向县令告状，替我除了妖僧，让我能够逃脱他的控制。听说阿爸你的儿子去世了，我愿意做你的儿子。"

李化惊讶地说："我是人，你是鬼，我们是两个世界的，怎么能成为父子呢？而且我没有生你养你，也承受不了你的孝顺，若你真的是鬼，也想报答我的恩情，能否帮我看看我的儿子珠儿去阴间过得好不好呢？"

小孩儿问："珠儿死了几天了？"听到李化说不到七天时，小孩儿又说："天气寒冷，尸体不会腐败。阿爸打开棺材看看尸体有没有损坏，如果没有的话，我有办法让珠儿活过来。"

After he was pushed to the ground, he didn't cry, instead, he calmly got up and said to Li Hua, "Dad, why did you do this?" After saying it, he climbed back onto the bed.

Li Hua was scared and fled from the room. He hid in the room where his wife was, and closed the door, leaving the boy outside. But when he turned around, the boy was already standing by his leg. Li Hua asked the boy, with a trembling voice, what he wanted and why he called him "Dad." The boy explained, "I'm from Suzhou. My surname is Zhan. When I was six years old, I was playing outside my home when an evil monk abducted and killed me. He buried me under a mulberry tree. Then he used sorcery to control my spirit and forced me to assist him in harming people. Thankfully, you, Dad, reported him to the county magistrate and got rid of the evil monk for me, which allowed me to escape his control. I heard that your son passed away. I wish to become your son."

Li Hua was astonished and said, "I'm human, and you're a ghost. We belong to two different worlds. How can we be father and son? Moreover, I didn't give you life or raise you, I can't accept your filial piety. If you are really a ghost and want to repay my kindness, could you help me check on my son Zhu'er in the underworld and see if he is doing well there?"

The boy asked, "How many days has it been since Zhu'er passed?" Upon hearing less than seven days, the boy said, "In this cold weather, the body won't decay. Dad, open the coffin to see whether the body has decayed. If it hasn't, then I have a way to bring Zhu'er back to life."

李化很高兴，立刻让人去刨坟，看到珠儿的尸体没有受到任何损伤。小孩儿让他把珠儿的尸体扛回家，放到床上，第二天就能看出效果。说完，这小孩儿就消失了。李化把珠儿的尸体扛回家，放到床上。第二天一早，珠儿果然睁开眼睛复活了。

大家很高兴珠儿死而复生。只是复活后的珠儿和之前大不一样，他变得聪明灵巧，一点不像之前那样痴呆了。但是，当到了晚上，珠儿睡着的时候，会僵卧着不动，也不翻身，一点儿鼻息都没有，仿佛死了一样。李化和家人们都很惊愕，以为珠儿又死了。但天快亮时，珠儿再次睁开了眼睛，眼睛里泛着聪慧的光芒。李化用借口将家人支走，然后向珠儿问道："说实话，你不是珠儿，而是那个詹姓小孩儿附身在珠儿身上，对不对？"

小孩儿回答："阿爸果然聪明。我本想在珠儿的阴魂过奈何桥之前拦住他，让他返生，但是没赶得及，珠儿已经过了奈何桥，忘了今世了。他与阿爸没有父子缘分。阿爸何不收留我？让我借珠儿的身体用一用。只要不驱赶我，过了七七四十九天，我就能和这躯体彻底合二为一，成为正常的人了。"

Li Hua was overjoyed. He immediately asked for the grave to be dug up and saw Zhu'er's body had no damage. The boy instructed him to bring the body home and place it on the bed, saying he would see the result the next day. After saying that, the boy disappeared. Li Hua carried Zhu'er's body back home and put it on the bed. Early the next morning, Zhu'er indeed opened his eyes and came back to life.

Everyone was delighted that Zhu'er had been resurrected. However, after the resurrection, Zhu'er seemed to be very different from before. He became intelligent and nimble, nothing like his former mentally challenged state. Yet at night, when Zhu'er slept, he would lie stiffly motionless, not even turning over. There was no sight of breathing, as if dead. Li Hua and his family were dumbfounded, thinking that Zhu'er had once again died. However, just before dawn, Zhu'er opened his eyes again, gleaming with intelligence. Li Hua used an excuse to send his family away, then asked Zhu'er, "Tell me the truth. You are not Zhu'er, but rather that child with the surname Zhan, and you have possessed Zhu'er's body, right?"

The boy replied, "Dad, you're really smart. Originally, I wanted to stop Zhu'er from crossing the Naihe Bridge and bring him back to this world. But I did not arrive in time. Zhu'er had already crossed the Naihe Bridge and forgot this lifetime. He and Dad did not have father-son fate for a long time. Dad, Why don't you accept me? Allow me to use Zhu'er's body. As long as you don't expel me, after 49 days, I will be able to fully integrate with this body and become a normal person."

李化虽然觉得这有些不妥，但他非常思念儿子，再加上家里人也不知道他不是珠儿，李化不忍让家人再次伤心，他便答应了下来。之后，他像培养珠儿一样，请老师教这孩子读书。这孩子很聪明，也非常孝顺，尽心赡养李化和李化的两个老婆，一直到为他们送终。

本故事改编自《聊斋志异》，作者：蒲松龄（公元1610年-1715年）

Although Li Hua felt uneasy about it, he deeply missed his son. Additionally, since his family didn't know he wasn't Zhu'er, and Li Hua couldn't bear to cause them heartache once more, so he agreed. Afterward, he hired a teacher to educate the boy just as he would have for Zhu'er. The child was very bright and extremely filial. He took care of Li Hua and Li Hua's two wives wholeheartedly until their final days.

The story is an adaptation of a short story from *Strange Tales from a Chinese Studio* by author Pu Songling (1610-1715 BC).

【夭折 yāo zhé】

夭折表示的意思是：某个人在未成年的时候就死去。也可以比喻事情中途失败或者废止。

夭折 means a person dies before reaching adulthood. It can also be used metaphorically to describe the failure or cancellation of something in the middle of its development.

【阿爸 ā bà】

阿爸是江苏省和浙江省的一些地区对父亲的称呼，是一种方言。

阿爸 is a term used in some regions of Jiangsu and Zhejiang provinces to refer to one's dad. It is a local expression.

【破财免灾 pò cái miǎn zāi】

破财免灾是汉语中的一个常见俗语，它的意思是：破费了钱财，可以免除灾祸。可以用于在某人损失了财物后来安慰他的话，比如你的朋友丢了很多钱，我们可以安慰他说："别太难过，破财免灾嘛！"

破财免灾 is a common Chinese saying that means spending money can prevent disaster. It can be used to comfort someone who has lost money. For instance, if your friend lost a lot of money, we could comfort them by saying, "Don't be too upset. You have lost money, so now misfortune won't fall upon you!"

【附身 fù shēn】

附身是中国鬼神观里一种常见的说法，意思是某人的身体被其他的鬼魂所占据。本故事中的小孩儿鬼附身在了已经没有灵魂的躯体上，所以其实没有造成伤害。但是，很多故事中的附身，通常是恶鬼附在还活着的人身上，如果不能及时驱赶走恶鬼，那么恶鬼就可能会永远占据这个身体，从而造成该身体原有的主人的死亡。通常被附身的人会做出和平常不一样的举动，因为操纵他身体的是那个鬼魂。所以如果日常生活中，我们认识的人做出了他平时不太常做的事情，我们可以这样比喻地说他："你干嘛？被鬼附身啦？"

附身 is a common expression in Chinese ghost and spirit beliefs where a person's body is possessed by another spirit. In this story, the ghost of the little boy possessed a body that no longer had a soul and, therefore, did not actually cause any harm. However, body possession in many stories usually involves an evil spirit taking over a living person's body. If the evil spirit is not expelled from the body in time, the evil spirit could possess the body permanently, which would lead to the death of the original owner of the body. Normally, a possessed person behaves differently than usual since the one controlling the body is the evil spirit. As a result, in everyday life, if someone we know does something out of character, we can metaphorically say, "What's wrong with you? Are you possessed by a ghost?"

【奈何桥 nài hé qiáo】

在中国民间神话传说中，奈何桥，是一个人死后，他的灵魂转世投胎时一定会经过的地点。在奈何桥旁边有一位叫做孟婆的女子，她负责给每个要投胎的鬼魂一碗汤，叫做孟婆汤，喝了这碗汤的鬼魂就会忘记全部的事情，然后投胎到下一世。

In Chinese folklore and mythology, 奈何桥 (Naihe Bridge) is a place a soul must cross after death before reincarnation. Next to the Naihe Bridge is a woman named Meng Po, who is responsible for giving each soul a bowl of soup, known as Meng Po Soup. Once the soul drinks the soup, the soul will forget everything and then reincarnate to the next life.

【七七四十九天 qī qī sì shí jiǔ tiān】

七个七天等于四十九天。七七四十九天是旧时汉族丧葬习俗里非常重要的一个概念。在一个人死后，他的家人们会每隔七天为他祭奠一次，一共祭奠七次。他死后的第七天叫做头七，第十四天叫做二七，以此类推，还有三七，四七，五七，六七，末七。每个祭奠日都会有不同的祭奠活动。

七七四十九天 (seven times seven days equals forty-nine days) is an important concept in ancient funeral customs of the Han ethnic group in China. After a person dies, their family holds a memorial service every seven days, seven times in total. The seventh day after death is called 头七 (the first seven), the fourteenth day is 二七 (the second seven), and so on. Following the same pattern, we have 三七 (the third seven), 四七 (the fourth seven), 五七 (the fifth seven), 六七 (the sixth seven), and 末七 (the final seven). There are different ritual activities on each day of the ceremony.

↑ 在敦煌壁画手稿中，我们能清晰地看到"二七亡人渡奈何"的字样，以及奈何桥上疑似"孟婆"的女子形象。

本插图选自《佛说十王经》，伯希和敦煌手稿，现藏于法国国家图书馆。

这个祭奠习俗是受到佛教的影响，因为在佛教的轮回转世观念中，人死后在七七四十九天之内，要经过阎王的七次审判，死者活着的家人如果在这期间为他念经超度，就能让他消灾免祸，投个好胎。而过了第四十九天，死者就会彻底与这一世断绝联系，去接受惩罚或者投胎去了。

This ceremonial custom was influenced by Buddhism. According to the Buddhist belief in reincarnation, within forty-nine days after a person's death, the deceased undergoes seven judgments by King Yan. If the living family members of the deceased perform rituals during this period, they can help the deceased avoid calamities and attain a better reincarnation. After forty-nine days, the deceased will completely sever ties with this lifetime and move on to receive punishment or reincarnate.

【送终 sòng zhōng】

送终指的是在亲属快要去世时在身边照顾他以及在他死后为他办理葬礼等事宜。

送终 refers to caring for a relative as they approach death and making arrangements for their funeral and other related matters after they pass away.

投胎

Reincarnation

本页插图选自《冬日婴戏图》，北宋 苏汉臣 绘，现藏于台北故宫博物院。

山西曲沃县县尉孙缅家最近不太太平，由于孙缅的外公去世，孙缅家大办丧事，葬礼一共持续了三天，前来吊唁的人络绎不绝。第四天下葬后，门庭若市的孙府终于安静下来。然而，就在下葬后那个晚上，孙缅家闹鬼的传闻却不胫而走，成为了曲沃县所有人家茶余饭后的谈资。

这传闻中的主角是孙缅的母亲，大家都叫她孙夫人。在给孙夫人的父亲举办葬礼的这三天里，孙夫人一直睡不好，因为她总会梦到各种妖魔鬼怪。

第一天晚上她梦到了一个红发鬼。那鬼留着一头红色的长发，浑圆的眼睛里也泛着红色的光芒，好像两颗正在燃烧的火球。他一手拿着铁叉，一手拿着根绳子，从窗户一下子跨进屋里来，拿起供品，坐在地上，大吃特吃起来。吃完后，他用绳子拴住孙夫人的父亲，拉着他走了。孙夫人看到父亲被拉走很着急，她大声呼唤着父亲，然后就从梦中惊醒了。

The home of Sun Mian, the county officer of Quwo County in the Shanxi Province, had not been very peaceful lately. Due to the passing of Sun Mian's grandfather, the family held a grand funeral that lasted for three days, with a continuous stream of people coming to pay their respects and offering their condolences. On the fourth day, after the burial, the once bustling Sun residence finally quieted down. However, that same evening, the rumor of ghosts appearing in Sun Mian's house spread quickly throughout Quwo County, becoming the topic of conversation for every family in Quwo County during their tea and meal times.

The protagonist of this rumor was Sun Mian's mother, whom everyone called Madam Sun. During the three days of Madam Sun's father's funeral, Madam Sun couldn't sleep well, as she constantly dreamed of various demons and ghosts.

On the first night, she dreamt of a red-haired ghost. That ghost had long red hair, and his round eyes glowed with a red light, like two burning fireballs. He held an iron trident in one hand, and a rope in the other. He leaped easily into the room through the window, grabbed some offerings, sat on the ground, and devoured them voraciously. After eating, he tied Madam Sun's father with the rope and dragged him away. Madam Sun, seeing her father being taken away, became anxious and called out to him loudly. Then she was startled awake from her dream.

第二天晚上，孙夫人感到屋里太热，就坐在门口纳凉，突然感到冷风飒飒，远处有人影掠过，她仔细看过去，看到院子里跳进来一个少女，她身姿曼妙，在院子里翩翩起舞，跳着跳着又进来一位少女，也跟着跳了起来。孙夫人感到非常不悦，在办丧事的家里怎能如此妖娆地跳舞呢？这是对丧主的大不敬。她开口大声呵斥两个陌生少女。她们两个听到后，盘着的头发刷的一声散开，美丽的脸庞变成了骷髅，尖叫着向孙夫人冲来。孙夫人吓得身体一抖，从床上翻身掉到了地上，她这才意识到刚才是自己做了一个噩梦，她一直躺在床上，未曾出门纳凉。

孙缅得知母亲两天晚上都受噩梦困绕，便在第三天晚上，差遣一位家奴去陪伴她，这位家奴带着自己六岁的女儿一同前往。话说这个六岁的小女孩儿，长相甜美，行动敏捷，像一只可爱的狸花猫，很招大人喜爱。只是她六岁了却依然不开口说话，孙夫人倍感惋惜，要不是她这哑巴的毛病，长大后是能许配给个好人家的。晚上有两人陪伴在屋内，孙夫人放心地睡着了。梦里，她梦到了父亲，看到父亲在地府接受审判，然后又看到父亲前往奈何

On the second night, Madam Sun felt it was too hot inside the house, so she sat by the door to cool off. Suddenly, she felt a chill wind and saw a shadowy figure in the distance. She looked closely and saw a young girl leap into the courtyard. The girl had a graceful figure and began dancing elegantly in the yard. As she danced, another young girl joined her and started dancing. Madam Sun was extremely displeased. How could anyone dance so seductively in a house holding a funeral? It was highly disrespectful to the deceased. She reproached loudly at the two unknown girls. Upon hearing her, their neatly tied hair suddenly unraveled, and their beautiful faces transformed into skulls. Screaming, they rushed toward Madam Sun. Terrified, Madam Sun jolted awake and fell from the bed to the floor. It was then she realized that she just had a nightmare. She had been lying in bed the entire time and had not gone outside to cool off.

Sun Mian, upon learning that his mother had been troubled by nightmares two nights in a row, so on the third night, he sent a household servant to accompany her. This servant brought her six-year-old daughter along with her. It was said that the little six-year-old girl was sweet-looking and agile, like an adorable Dragon Li cat. Many adults adored her. However, although she was already six years old, she still didn't speak. Madam Sun felt deeply regretful about this. If she didn't have the problem of muteness, she would have been able to marry into a good family when she grew up. With two people accompanying her in the room that night, Madam Sun fell asleep peacefully. In her dream, she dreamed of her father. She saw her fath-

桥，接过孟婆汤，在喝下汤之前朝着她的方向摆了摆手，似乎在向她告别，孙夫人非常伤心，忍不住呜咽了起来。家奴听到孙夫人哭泣的声音，赶紧过去轻声将其叫醒。

第四天，下葬日，孙缅请了多位高僧诵经，目的是送亡魂最后一程，也为了为孙夫人祈福，希望她晚上不要再被噩梦缠身。所有仪式结束后，孙夫人回到自己的房间，在桌子上看到一个破旧的物品，她拿起来端详，忽然像想起来什么一样，大叫一声，晕厥倒地。

家奴听到孙夫人的叫声就前去查看，发现她晕倒在地上，立刻禀告给孙缅，后者急忙请来了医生。医生赶来时，孙夫人已经幽幽地醒来了，医生为其诊脉，发现孙夫人是受到了惊吓，便询问其受到惊吓的缘由。孙夫人指着桌子上的玩意儿询问道："这东西是谁拿来的？"众人纷纷表示不知道。孙缅拿起那东西，发现它是一个布老虎，虽然做工精良，布料颜色鲜艳，但已经非常陈旧，还破了几个洞，好像被搁置了几十年。他向母亲询问这是什么东西。孙夫人叹了口气，娓娓道来。

er being judged in the underworld, then she saw her father heading to the Naihe Bridge where he took the Meng Po Soup. Before drinking it, he waved in her direction as if saying goodbye. Madam Sun was extremely saddened and couldn't help but sob. The servant heard Madam Sun's cries, quickly went over, and gently woke her.

On the fourth day, the day of the burial, Sun Mian invited several prominent monks to chant sutras, hoping to send off the soul of the deceased on his last journey and also pray for Madam Sun, wishing she would no longer be troubled by nightmares. After all the rituals were completed, Madam Sun returned to her room and saw an old item on the table. She picked it up to examine it, and suddenly, she seemed to have remembered something, she let out a scream, fainted, and fell to the ground.

Hearing Madam Sun's scream, the servant went to check and found her unconscious on the floor. She immediately reported to Sun Mian, and he quickly called for a doctor. By the time the doctor arrived, Madam Sun had already regained consciousness. The doctor examined her pulse and found that she had been frightened. He then asked what had scared her. Madam Sun pointed at the item on the table and asked, "Who brought this?" Everyone claimed they didn't know. Sun Mian picked up the item and found it to be a cloth tiger, finely made with brightly colored fabric but very old and with several holes, as if it had been left for decades. He asked his mother what the object was. Madam Sun sighed and began to explain.

原来这布老虎是孙夫人小时候最喜欢的玩具。经常抱在怀里，爱不释手。有一次，在和父亲玩捉迷藏的游戏时，她不小心遗失了这布老虎，府上几十人一起寻找，也没能找到。在父亲死后，这布老虎却突然冒了出来。孙夫人本来以为，她这几天是在做噩梦，但看到这只属于她和父亲的回忆的玩具出现在房间里，孙夫人惊觉她这几天的经历应该都是真实的，并非梦境，回想起她看到的可怕鬼怪们，她吓得昏厥了过去。

屋里的人听完这些话，都面面相觑，不知作何反应。随后，孙府闹鬼的传闻迅速传遍了曲沃县。孙缅作为县尉，并不完全相信鬼神之事，他觉得这事情有蹊跷，在送走医生后，他叫来在孙府做事的家奴们，一一审问，想要调查出白天有谁进过孙夫人的房间。很快，有人说看到那个哑巴小女孩儿从孙夫人的房间跑出来。

孙缅派人叫来小女孩儿，同时，他担心带刀的衙役们吓到小孩儿，让她无法供出幕后主使，便让衙役们都到屋外等待，屋里只剩下孙缅，孙夫人和哑巴小女孩

It turned out that the cloth tiger was her favorite toy when she was young. She used to hold it all the time and loved it so dearly that she couldn't separate herself from it. Once, while playing hide-and-seek with her father, she accidentally lost it. Despite dozens of people searching the house together, they couldn't find it. After her father's death, the cloth tiger suddenly appeared. Madam Sun initially thought she had been having nightmares for the last couple of days. But seeing the appearance of this toy in her room, a memory that belonged to her and her father, she suddenly realized that her recent experiences might have been real, not dreams. Remembering the terrifying ghosts she had seen, she fainted from fear.

After hearing this, everyone in the room was stunned and didn't know how to react. Subsequently, the rumor that ghosts appeared in the Sun residence spread rapidly throughout Quwo County. Sun Mian, the county officer, didn't completely believe in ghosts and spirits. He thought there was something suspicious. After sending off the doctor, he summoned the servants who worked in the Sun residence and questioned them one by one, trying to figure out who had entered Madam Sun's room during the day. Soon, someone mentioned seeing the mute girl running out of Madam Sun's room.

Sun Mian sent for the little girl. At the same time, worried that armed constables might frighten the child and prevent her from revealing the mastermind, he had them wait outside the room, leaving only Sun Mian, Madam Sun, and the mute girl inside.

儿。孙缅问她是不是她把布老虎拿进房间的？小女孩儿点了点头，孙缅又问她是她母亲让她拿进来的吗？小女孩儿摇了摇头。孙缅又问了几个人是否是主使，小女孩儿都摇头。孙缅看软的不好使，便威胁说要将小女孩儿的母亲捉起来关进牢里，小女孩儿着急地一把抓住孙夫人的衣角，突然，开口说话了："夫人！你还记不记得你小的时候收养了一只狸花猫？一只耳朵上有打架留下的缺口。"孙夫人有些吃惊，点头说是的。

"夫人，我就是那只狸花猫啊！当年我不想被束缚，就从你家逃了出来，我逃走后，还听到过你在后院哭泣着寻找我。两年后，我死了，见到了阎王，他让我投胎成人，但却投胎到了乞丐家里，我常年吃不饱饭，不到二十岁就又死了，再次去到地府，阎王看我在饥寒交迫时也没有做偷鸡摸狗之事，便把我投胎成您的家奴，这下不愁温饱了。我这已经是第三生了，夫人您却还在这儿，生活顺遂，可真是天大的福分呀！"

孙缅和孙夫人听了这段话都惊愕不已，一开始还不太相信，但是孙夫人又问了很多她小时候的事

Sun Mian asked if she had brought the cloth tiger into the room. The girl nodded. He then asked if her mother had instructed her to do so. The girl shook her head. Sun Mian asked the girl if any of the several people he mentioned were the instigators, and the girl shook her head each time. Realizing that the gentle approach was not working, he threatened to capture the girl's mother and imprison her. The girl, very anxious, grabbed the corner of Madam Sun's clothes and suddenly began to speak, "Madam! Do you remember when you were young, you adopted a Dragon Li cat with a notch on its ear from a fight?" Madam Sun was shocked and said yes as she nodded her head.

"Madam, I am that Dragon Li cat! Back then, I didn't want to be confined, so I ran away from your house. After escaping, I heard you crying and searching for me in the backyard. Two years later, I died and saw King Yan. He allowed me to reincarnate as a human, but I was reincarnated into a beggar's family. I often went hungry and died before I was twenty. Returning to the underworld again, King Yan saw that despite my extreme poverty, I had not stolen or committed petty theft, so he allowed me to reincarnate as your house servant. Now I no longer worry about food and clothing. This is my third life already, but you, Madam, are still here living a prosperous life. What a great fortune!"

Sun Mian and Madam Sun were astonished after hearing these words. At first, they didn't quite believe it, but Madam Sun asked many questions

情，小女孩儿都对答如流，不仅知道孙夫人小时候喜欢穿黄衣白裙，还了解她的所有玩具，让孙夫人不得不相信她。更重要的是根据小女孩儿所说，布老虎就是狸花猫叼走藏在院墙下面的洞穴里的。那晚她听到孙夫人呜咽着喊父亲，便把布老虎找了出来，想要安慰孙夫人。这下，一切就都说得通了。

过了那一晚，小女孩儿又变回从前的哑巴。许是上天觉得她未饮孟婆汤，还记得前世和地府的情形，所以不给她讲话的机会。不过，这不影响孙夫人对她的宠爱，就像宠爱小时候的狸花猫一样，对她爱护有加，直到她长大到十八岁，将她许配给了一个好人家，这辈子都不愁吃穿了。

本故事改编自唐代小说《广异记》，作者戴孚，生卒年代不详，《广异记》成书年代约为公元766至779年间。

about her childhood, which the girl answered accurately and flawlessly. She not only knew that Madam Sun liked to wear yellow clothes and white skirts but also knew all her toys, making it impossible for Madam Sun not to believe her. The most important evidence was that according to the girl, the cloth tiger had been taken by the Dragon Li cat and hidden in a hole under the courtyard wall. That night when she heard Madam Sun sobbing and calling for her father, she went and brought the cloth tiger to comfort Madam Sun. This explained everything.

After that night, the little girl returned to being mute. Perhaps the gods thought that she hadn't drunk the Meng Po Soup and remembered her past lives and what the underworld was like, so they didn't allow her to speak. However, this did not affect Madam Sun's affection for her. Just as she had doted on her Dragon Li cat when she was little, she showered her with love and care until she grew up to be eighteen years old. Then, she arranged a marriage for her to a good family, ensuring that she would never have to worry about food or clothing in this lifetime.

This story is adapted from the Tang Dynasty novel *Great Book of Marvels* by author Dai Fu, whose birth and death dates are unknown. The book *Great Book of Marvels* was completed approximately between 766 and 779 AD.

【县尉 xiàn wèi】

县尉是古代的一种官名，相当于现在的警察局局长。

县尉 was an official title in ancient times, equivalent to a police chief today.

【吊唁 diào yàn】

去到死者家里，祭奠死者并安慰其家属的行为叫做吊唁。

The act of going to the deceased's home to pay respects to the deceased and comfort their family is called 吊唁.

【门庭若市 mén tíng ruò shì】

门庭若市是一个成语，其中"庭"的意思是"庭院"。这个成语的意思是：门前和院子里好像集市一样热闹，形容来到家里的客人很多，非常热闹。

门庭若市 is an idiom in which 庭 means courtyard. This idiom means that the area in front of the door and the courtyard are as bustling as a market, describing a situation where many guests have come to the house, making it very lively.

【不胫而走 bú jìng ér zǒu】

不胫而走是一个成语，其中"胫"的意思是"小腿"。这个成语的意思是：消息没有腿但却能跑，即消息传播迅速。

不胫而走 is an idiom in which 胫 means leg. This idiom means that news, although it has no legs, can still run, implying that information spreads quickly.

【供品 gòng pǐn】

在民间宗教习俗中，用来供奉佛祖，神仙和祖先所用的物品的统称叫做供品。食物类的供品一般是葬礼中最常见的一种，比如有五谷杂粮，肉类，水果，糖果，酒水等。

In folk religious customs, items used to offer to Buddha, deities, and ancestors are collectively called 供品 (offerings). Food offerings are generally the most common at funerals, such as different grains, meat, fruits, sweets, water, liquor, etc.

人们认为一个人刚死后，他的灵魂还没有转世，还可能在人间逗留一段时间，之后才会前往阴间，那么葬礼上的食物将会是他离开这个世界前的最后一顿饭，家人们会尽可能地为他摆上所有的美食。食物的种类和份量都有讲究，因为除了死者要享用，来接死者的阴间差役们也可能会吃这些食物。另外，还有一种说法就是，因为各种理由而没有去阴间的孤魂野鬼们，也会来吃这些供品。所以，才会经常有故事或者传说讲到在葬礼上看见鬼。

People believe that after a person has just died, their soul has not yet reincarnated and may linger in the human world for a while before moving on to the underworld. Thus, the food at the funeral will be their last meal before leaving this world, and the family will try their best to provide all kinds of delicacies for them. The types and quantities of food are important because, in addition to the deceased enjoying them, the underworld messengers who come to fetch the deceased might also eat these offerings. Additionally, there is another belief that wandering spirits who, for various reasons, have not gone to the underworld might also come to eat these offerings. This is why there are often stories or legends about seeing ghosts at funerals.

【家奴 jiā nú】

在封建社会里，官员和富人家里干活的奴隶们就叫做家奴。

In feudal society, slaves who worked in the homes of officials and wealthy families were called 家奴.

【狸花猫 lí huā māo】

狸花猫是原产于中国的一个猫的品种。在中国古代，富人家就已经有了把猫当作宠物来养的习惯。

The Chinese Li Hua, also known as Dragon Li, is a breed of cat native to China. In ancient China, wealthy families already had the habit of keeping cats as pets.

◄ 在这幅古画中，颜色较深的那只猫就是狸花猫。

本插图选自《耄耋图》，宋朝皇帝 宋徽宗真迹，现藏于台北故宫博物院。

【许配 xǔ pèi】

在中国古代，由父母做主，将女儿嫁给某人的行为就叫做许配。比如在故事二《画皮》中，贪图钱财的父母，就将自己年轻的女儿许配给一个有钱的老头儿。

In ancient China, the act of parents deciding to marry their daughter to someone was called 许配. For example, in story 2 "The Ghost with Painted Skin," the greedy parents betrothed their young daughter to a wealthy old man.

【布老虎 bù lǎo hǔ】

布老虎是用布做的老虎，是一种古代就已在中国民间流传的手工艺品，是很多孩子们的玩具，也可以当作室内的摆设。

布老虎 is a tiger made of cloth, a popular traditional folk craft in ancient China. It was a toy for many children and could also be used as interior decoration.

【捉迷藏 zhuō mí cáng】

捉迷藏是一种民间游戏，多人按照规则躲起来，让一个人去寻找躲藏的人们。在唐代就有关于这个游戏的文字记载。

捉迷藏 is a folk game where multiple people hide according to the rules, and one person searches for those who are hiding. There are written records of this game dating back to the Tang Dynasty.

【面面相觑 miàn miàn xiāng qù】

面面相觑是一个成语，其中"觑"的意思是"看"。面面相觑就是：互相对着看。用来形容因为紧张，惊讶或者尴尬而不知所措的样子。

面面相觑 is an idiom in which 觑 means to look. 面面相觑 means looking at each other. It is used to describe a situation where people are unsure what to do due to nervousness, surprise, or embarrassment.

【阎王 yán wang】

阎王，又称阎罗王，阎罗，他是中国民间信仰里，管理地狱的神。"阎王"这个词其实是从梵语中音译过来的词汇，本意是"捆绑"，在梵语中表达的是"捆绑有罪的人"。而阎王管理地狱这个观点，是佛教从古代印度传入中国后，和中国本土宗教道教互相影响，而演变出来的带有汉化色彩的观念。

阎王 (King Yan), also known as 阎罗王 and 阎罗, is a deity in Chinese folk religious belief who rules over hell. The term 阎王 is actually a transliteration from Sanskrit, originally meaning "to bind." In Sanskrit, it referred to "binding the guilty." The concept of King Yan ruling the underworld emerged through the interaction of Buddhism, which was brought to China from ancient India, with China's native Taoist religion. This interaction gave rise to a syncretic notion with Han ethnic characteristics.

↑ 在敦煌壁画手稿中，我们能清晰地看到"阎罗王"的字样，坐在桌子前的就是阎王。他正在审判死后来到阴间的亡魂们。画中的镜子准确反映亡人前生的行为。说明亡人在生的行为均被记录在案，如果做了坏事还想侥幸逃过阎王审判是不可能的。

本插图选自《佛说十王经》，伯希和敦煌手稿，现藏于法国国家图书馆。

【偷鸡摸狗 tōu jī mō gǒu】

偷鸡摸狗是一个成语。字面意思是："偷了一只鸡，又偷了一只狗。"用来指小偷小摸的偷窃行为。

偷鸡摸狗 is an idiom. The literal meaning is "stole a chicken and then stole a dog." It is used to refer to petty theft.

【对答如流 duì dá rú liú】

对答如流是一个成语，表示回答问题时毫不犹豫，回答地像流水一样流畅。也可以用来比喻某个人思维敏捷，口才好。

对答如流 is an idiom that means answering questions without hesitation, as smoothly as flowing water. It can also be used to describe someone who is quick-witted and articulate.

Bibliography

Book from the Eastern Jin Dynasty (317-420):

《搜神记》，甘宝

In Search of the Supernatural. Author: Gan Bao.
The Tree Demon (Story 9), *Underworld Official* (Story 12), and *Deceased Son Visits in Dream* (Story 13) are adapted from this book.

Books from the Tang Dynasty (618-907):

《酉阳杂俎》，段成式

Miscellaneous Morsels from Youyang. Author: Duan Chengshi.
The Lonely Wandering Soul (Story 5) is adapted from this book.

《玄怪录》，牛僧孺

Accounts of Mysteries and Monsters. Author: Niu Sengru.
The Water Demon (Story 10) is adapted from this book.

《广异记》，戴孚

Great Book of Marvels. Author: Dai Fu.
Reincarnation (Story 15) is adapted from this book.

Books from the Song Dynasty (960-1279):

《太平广记》，李昉等人共同汇编

Extensive Records of the Taiping Era. It is a collection of stories compiled by Li Fang and others.
The Vengeful Spirit (Story 6) is adapted from this book.

《梦溪笔谈》，沈括

Dream Pool Essays. Author: Shen Kuo.
Zhong Kui Kills Ghosts (Story 7) is adapted from this book.

Books from the Qing Dynasty (1636-1912):

《聊斋志异》，蒲松龄

Strange Tales from a Chinese Studio. Author: Pu Songling.
The Ghost Pressing Down on the Bed (Story 1), *The Ghost with Painted Skin* (Story 2), *The Fox Spirit* (Story 8), and *Body Possession* (Story 14) are adapted from this book.

《淞隐漫录》，王韬

Jottings from Carefree Travel. Author: Wang Tao.
Hanba the Drought Demon (Story 4) is adapted from this book.

《子不语》，袁枚

What Master Confucius Does Not Speak Of. Author: Yuan Mei.
Soul Snatching (Story 11) is adapted from this book.

Color Illustrations and Audio of the Stories

To view the illustrations in color and download the audio of the stories, visit the following link:
ALLanguageCafe.com/ChineseGhostStories

Copyright Information for the Illustrations in This Book
Most of the illustrations in this book are from ancient paintings that are already in the public domain. You can visit the link above to check the sources of these paintings and find out in which museums they are exhibited.

Additionally, the illustration on page 126 is a photograph taken by

Extensive Grading Process for Classifying Our Stories at the Right Level

Starter Level	Basic Level	Intermediate Level	Advanced Level	Mastery Level
(HSK 1 - HSK 2)	(HSK 2 - HSK 3)	(HSK 3 - HSK 4)	(HSK 4 - HSK 5)	(HSK 5 - HSK 6)

Engaging Materials - Covering a Range of Topics

Travel — Chinese Idioms — Daily Life

Myth & Legends — Family & Relationships — School Life

Horror & Suspense — Chinese Culture — Fairy Tales & Fantasy

To purchase Chinese Graded Readers with pinyin and English translation, visit the following link:
ALLanguageCafe.com/ShortStories

17167728R00096